Sonata Summer

Ann Ulrich Miller

Sonata Summer

Ann Ulrich Miller

Earth Star Publications
Pagosa Springs, Colorado

FIRST EDITION
First Printing June 2012
Second Printing July 2018

Library of Congress Control Number: 2012937409

Earth Star Publications
Eckert, Colorado

Please check www.earthstarpublications.com
for updated address information.

ISBN 978-0-944851-35-7

Printed in the United States of America

Cover photo by Jon Barnes
www.ultimatetaxi.com
Author photo on cover by Doug Elmore

Foreword

My appreciation goes to all of my friends and colleagues who lived and worked in Aspen during the late '70s and early '80s.

When I arrived in the Rocky Mountains barely at the age of 26 with my husband and our toddler son, it was as though a whole new world opened up for me—and actually, that is precisely what my spirit guides had in mind.

I am grateful to my friend Belinda, who took the chance and hired me as a proofreader at the *Aspen Times*. I learned a lot working there and experienced Aspen through a local's eyes. Through getting to know the community—which was unlike any place I'd ever lived before—I discovered the wonderful cultural aspects, along with the beauty of the surrounding mountains and public lands.

I'm grateful to Jeff, my first husband, whose career began at the Aspen Ranger District and its multitude of great people.

Winning a full scholarship to the Aspen Writers Conference in 1982 was an honor that inspired me to develop my writing abilities and pushed me forward with confidence and enthusiasm.

This novel came about because of my infatuation with Aspen and the Roaring Fork Valley. Visitors see, perhaps, only the glamor and excitement of a resort community made famous because of celebrities or out-of-your-reach housing prices. I hope they will be able to see another view of Aspen—through the eyes of a working class local—in *Sonata Summer*.

Ann Ulrich Miller

Other Books by Ann Ulrich Miller

Rainbow Majesty

Throughout All Time, A Cosmic Love Story

Stepping Forth, An American Girl Coming of Age in the '60s

The Dream Chasers

Under the name Ann Carol Ulrich

Intimate Abduction

Return To Terra

The Light Being

Night of the November Moon

Young Adult Fiction

The Mystery at Hickory Hill

The Secret of the Green Paint

The Pouting Pumpkin Mystery

The Legend of the Lantern

In the Shadow of the Tower

The Ground Hog Mystery

Spring Break at the Lake House

Pre-Teen Fiction

The Root Cellar Mystery

Visit www.AnnUlrichMiller.com

Aspen

*A*spen, Colorado is a former silver-mining town with a summertime population of 20,000. Surrounded by spectacular mountains and rivers, clean air and abundant sunshine, along with its charming Victorian downtown, Aspen serves as a retreat from life's stresses as well as a place to grow—personally, artistically, and spiritually.

You will find music and musicians everywhere. Artist-faculty, staff, students and guest artists frequent the restaurants or stroll down the wide pedestrian malls. Hiking through fields of wildflowers, biking amid incredible vistas, or just spending time quietly in the beautiful environment soothes the soul.

At an altitude of 7,900 feet, summer days in Aspen are generally dry and sunny with temperatures in the 80s, while nights are clear and cool.

The Aspen Music Festival and School, founded in 1949, is an internationally renowned classical music festival that presents music in an intimate, small-town setting. It is a training ground for young adult musicians.

The Festival and School was founded by Elizabeth and Walter Paepcke of Chicago and is rooted in the idea that it is the combination of art and nature that fosters the growth of the human spirit. This guiding principle still informs every aspect of the organization. Substantial artistic collaboration was provided by Henri Temianka and his Paganini Quartet during the festival's formative years.

More than 350 classical music events take place in eight weeks every summer, from July to August, with up to eight events a day and more than 100,000 patrons participating.

Music students receive a combination of classroom and performance experiences. A broad curriculum includes playing in an orchestra, individual lessons, master classes and recitals, with 750 students in attendance.

For more information visit ***www.aspenmusicfestival.com***

Sonata Summer

1

*R*hea Sinclair stood in the express lane, arms laden with groceries. Cash registers beeped all around her. Clerks, dressed in bulky orange smocks, didn't have time to notice the impatient frowns on customers' faces as the lanes filled in the late afternoon rush.

She had been on her way home when she remembered to stop at the market for some Monterey Jack cheese. Somehow she had ended up with a half dozen other essentials. Rhea's arm ached as she struggled to hold onto a half-gallon of milk, a stalk of celery, the cheese and the rest. She could feel the plastic bag containing the celery slipping.

What was taking so long? Was some ignorant moron using coupons in *this*—the *express* lane? A peek over the shoulder of the man in front of Rhea revealed this very fact. A fat lady in a gaudy blouse and wide pink pants had a pile of cut-outs to give to the poor cashier. "Turkey!" Rhea hissed under her breath.

As she sighed in futility, Rhea caught someone staring at her. In the next line a man's gaze seemed to reach out and draw her toward him. A smile played on his lips and his brown eyes took her in.

Caught off guard, Rhea turned away. After a moment, she glanced at him and noticed his muddy, sweat-soaked T-shirt. Filthy jeans clung to his thin waist and flared out over a pair of well-worn, mud-covered cowboy boots. He had brown arms, broad shoulders and a tanned, muscular neck. Beneath spiky reddish-brown hair and dirt, he was actually attractive.

He must have sensed her observations, for he turned to look at her once again, this time sweeping Rhea from head to toe with those dark eyes that seemed to penetrate her very soul. She immediately diverted her gaze and felt a cold surge of panic rise within her. Pounding swelled inside her chest. She didn't realize that the line was moving until the person behind her tapped her on the shoulder.

"Miss... you're next."

Rhea jerked as the voice behind her spoke. She noticed the clerk waiting and set her burdens down in relief. The cash register beeped as it recorded each item. The bag boy stuffed it all into Rhea's cloth bag while the checker murmured the total.

Aware of those brown eyes fixed on her again, Rhea fumbled through her backpack for her money. She knew that *she* was now the "turkey." The smooth, white, tapered tips of her fingers trembled, and she dropped the change onto the floor.

Somebody in line sighed impatiently as Rhea stooped to retrieve her coins. By the time she paid for her groceries and grabbed her pack and bag, the cowboy had left.

Rhea hurried outside the store to her bicycle at the racks. She balanced the groceries in the front basket, then swung her leg over, taking care that her long cotton skirt wouldn't catch in the spokes. Then she coasted out of the shopping center parking lot and began the climb up Mill Street.

Even in her sleeveless cotton shirt, she perspired as she pedaled past tourists in cars or on foot. The high temperature offered a sharp contrast to the cold she remembered from June of last year. Still, the dry heat was far more refreshing than the oppressive humidity of the Midwest, which—after almost twenty-eight years—she had left behind.

June usually wasn't this hot in Aspen. Last summer Rhea remembered June as a wet, rather cool month in the Rockies. Some cool mountain air would settle in by dark. This was one reason why she loved Colorado and had chosen to stay in Aspen after last fall.

She cherished the beauty and mystery of Aspen's surrounding mountains. They held her most cherished memories—despite the horrors of her life last September. She could never leave them —nor could she leave *him*.

In downtown Aspen, Rhea shared a second-story apartment with Mona Whitecloud, who was of Native American descent. Mona worked nights at Gustav's Restaurant, but tonight she had the evening off. Mona's straight black hair fell over her shoulders as she stepped into the kitchen, wearing a cream-colored halter that accentuated her plump figure.

"*Geez Louise*, it's stifling in here," complained Mona. "Let's go out and eat."

Rhea grabbed a hot pad and opened the oven door to check on dinner. "But I already baked your favorite quiche," said Rhea. "I'm afraid the oven made it hot in here."

"Well, in that case ... let's eat out on the balcony."

They took their filled plates onto the patio. Rhea welcomed the coolness that came with the evening air, but she didn't think much of the small balcony, because the gas station across the alley obscured the view of Aspen Mountain. Also, the constant rush of traffic noise came from Main Street one block away.

"This is scrumptious," said Mona. "You know, you ought to sell your recipe to Gustav."

"I'm glad you like it, Mona. But just because you work for the guy doesn't mean he'd want my recipe." She watched the setting sun play with the highlights of Mona Whitecloud's black hair and cast a warm glow on her bronze skin. Envy wasn't a part of her nature, but Rhea sometimes wished she shared the Native American roots that gave her roommate that beautiful coloring.

The ripple of a flute floated into the alley, catching their attention. The neighbor downstairs had begun a practice session. As though the music reminded her of something, Mona asked, "Did you register for classes yet?"

"Not yet," Rhea replied. "I'll do that Wednesday."

"Do you audition then, too?"

Rhea nodded. She listened to the flute's melody and imagined herself in a grassy meadow surrounded by columbines and distant snowy peaks. Wednesday she would register at the Aspen Music School, where she had been on scholarship last summer.

Mona set her plate down after she was finished and wiped her mouth with her napkin. "Hey, I've got a great idea. Let's go to the Smuggler tonight."

Rhea groaned. "No ... *you* go, if you want."

"Aw, come on, Rhea. You've been cooped up in this stuffy apartment all week, practicing the piano. You need a break."

Rhea sighed. "I know it's your night off, and I appreciate your concern, but ... I'm not interested." The last thing Rhea wanted was to have Mona drag her off to some bar. That was Mona's thing. Rhea hated bars.

"What's it gonna hurt? One drink at one bar. Come on. Please ... for me? Okay, Rhea?"

Rhea hated to hurt her roommate's feelings. Mona had been so patient during the past year, never bugging her when she insisted on being left alone. How often was it that Mona spent her precious evening off in Rhea's company?

"Well, how about it?" prompted Mona.

"I really should keep practicing..."

"The piano will still be here," insisted Mona.

Rhea hesitantly gave in, but the idea did not thrill her. "Just give me a few minutes to change clothes."

Mona did the dishes while Rhea went to her room. Rhea had the larger of the two bedrooms, only because it housed her Steinway piano. She could sit at the piano and view Bleeker Street and its array of well-kept Victorian houses, secluded by cotton-woods and well-groomed lawns. She stood before her closet and pondered which sun dress to wear. On impulse, she grabbed a sleeveless turquoise frock.

After she put it on, she went to the dresser and slid the brush through her long, honey-colored hair. She examined her face with the blueish-green eyes, slender nose and narrow shape of her face. In the mirror she discovered with sudden amazement how pale her skin was compared to Mona's rich tan. The long hours of practice indoors had taken their toll, the freckles dotting her arms and cheeks barely visible.

This is silly, Rhea thought to herself. *We're only going to a bar. What does it matter who sees me?* She was only going to please Mona, after all.

Dusk had settled in when they arrived at the Smuggler Bar in downtown Aspen. The walk from their apartment had revived Rhea's spirits. The climb down the stairwell to the tavern did not seem like such a dismal retreat into the unknown. Mona led her inside a dark, stuffy room, where they were greeted by smoke, loud country and western music, and beer smell. Even for this early hour, Rhea considered the place crowded.

"This is strictly a local's hangout," Mona explained. "Tourists don't usually come here." She nudged Rhea into a corner booth.

Rhea glanced around at both young and old faces. No one paid attention to her.

"Now, is this so bad?" asked Mona.

"Well, they could have better ventilation. And why is it so dark?"

A band of rowdy types at a table across the room snorted and roared with raucous laughter. Rhea noticed some of them wore cowboy hats. They surrounded two pitchers of beer, one half full. A couple of the cowboys had noticed Rhea and Mona in their corner and poked each other. Then one of them whistled.

The waitress appeared and took their order. Rhea requested a strawberry daiquiri while Mona ordered a beer.

"Ahh ... *Rhea Sinclair*," rang out a masculine voice.

Rhea turned to face a massive man in a white shirt. In a moment she recognized the large round head, short blond hair and glasses. She grinned. "Jerome—hello!" Swinging back to Mona, Rhea introduced her roommate. "Mona, I'd like you to meet Jerome Hodges, one of my friends from the Music School."

"Happy to meet you." Jerome extended a fat arm to Mona, and in his oafish fashion, knocked over a ketchup bottle. Pushing his thick glasses up further, he said, "Fancy meeting you here, Rhea. I just got into town today." Suddenly, a puzzled look crossed his pasty face. "I didn't think you were coming back this summer."

Rhea explained, "Actually, I've been in Aspen all year."

"Are you on scholarship again?"

Rhea shook her head. "Not this summer."

Jerome signaled to some friends at the bar. "Gotta go. Nice

to meet you, Moriah. Talk to you later, Rhea."

After he was gone, Mona scrunched up her forehead. "Who was *that*?"

Rhea suppressed a smile. Jerome was terrible at names, but his heart was in the right place. She explained how she had met him last summer, when they had enrolled in two of the same classes at the Music School. "He plays French horn," she said, "and he's very good."

The waitress brought their drinks. Rhea sipped at her daiquiri. It was too tart.

"He's not your type," Mona commented.

Rhea wiped her lips with the napkin. "Jerome and I are just friends, Mona. He's kind of like … my brother."

The table of cowboys started to get wild. They whooped and cheered, throwing out lewd remarks to anyone who passed by. The waitress went back and forth, undisturbed and distant. Rhea wouldn't have minded being in the bar except for this unruly bunch. She felt particularly vulnerable to their remarks and wondered how she and Mona were going to escape being their victims.

"You know, Rhea, I'm glad you're finally taking this first step," said Mona.

"What first step?"

"Facing the world. Coming out of your shell." Mona lowered her voice. "I've got to hand it to you. I truly admire you for not leaving Aspen after last fall. If I had been in your place …"

Mona's voice tapered off as Rhea noticed a familiar figure who had just joined the rowdy group of cowboys. Something pricked to life within her, causing her heart to flutter. It was the man she had seen in the grocery store earlier. He had changed into a clean western shirt and jeans, and his hair was combed. She was right. He was quite attractive. She studied his strong, slender body, the shoulders broad and well formed.

For a startling second, he caught her gaze. She quickly looked back at Mona, who was still rambling. "I can understand your wishing to keep his memory alive, Rhea. But it's hard having to explain to people who come over and see all those pictures of

Parker lying around. What am I supposed to tell them?"

Rhea hadn't been aware of the heavy ground Mona treaded. "I didn't know keeping pictures of Parker around bothered you, Mona."

"Don't be silly. It doesn't bother me, Rhea," said Mona. "It's just kind of ... of ... morbid."

Before Rhea could respond, she looked up and found the man from the grocery store standing over her. He smiled down at her and she smelled a mixture of odors—hay and leather, but mostly alcohol. He weaved a little.

"Hullo," he greeted her in a deep voice. His words slurred together as he asked, "Hey, haven't we met somewhere before?"

Mona took charge of the situation. "As if you couldn't think of a better line than that! Get lost, jerk!"

Rhea knew it wasn't a line, but she didn't say anything

Stifling a burp, the man backed away from them. Insults came from the table across the room. "Struck out, eh?" and, "That's what you get when you stick around horses all day!" They laughed at him, only Rhea was the one who felt embarrassed. Heat rose to her cheeks as she stared into her drink.

"Why are you blushing?" Mona picked up her glass and drank. "Don't let it get to you."

Rhea sipped her daiquiri. She didn't want to act like a fool in front of Mona, who was composed and self-assured at all times. But her hand trembled as she set the glass down.

"You really are a bundle of nerves," said Mona.

"Who was he?" Rhea asked in a low voice. "Do you know him?"

"I've seen him around." Mona scanned the table of cowboys. "His name is Trey Michaels. Unless I'm mistaken, he works out at the Nickelson Creek Ranch."

Rhea understood the grubby appearance now. Apparently, when she had seen him in the market, he had just gotten off work.

"Hey, you're *interested* in him, aren't you?" Mona grinned at her.

"No way," said Rhea. "He's not my type."

"Well, who *is* your type?"

Before Rhea could reply, Trey Michaels staggered toward their table once more. He grinned, revealing straight white teeth. His face flushed, he pointed a finger at Rhea. "I remembered," he drawled. "The girl at the market. I knew I'd seen you somewhere."

Rhea glanced at Mona, who watched with an amused smile. Obviously, Rhea was expected to fight her own battle this round.

"Hey ... let me buy you a drink," Trey continued. "Whyn't you and your friend ..." He beckoned toward the table of cowboys, who had quieted down and watched them, hanging on every word.

Rhea couldn't stand another second. She grabbed her backpack and stood up to leave.

"But ... wait ..." Trey Michaels stood there, trying to keep his balance.

Rhea didn't wait for Mona. She stalked past the jeering cowboys and didn't stop until she was outside the tavern. There she greeted the fresh air and coolness of the evening.

"Rhea!" Mona caught up and together they climbed the stairs to the street. "We didn't finish our drinks."

"I need to go home," Rhea muttered. "You can stay, if you want."

With a sigh, Mona shook her head and returned to the bar. Rhea walked the six blocks home. Her mind was in a turmoil. The encounter with Trey Michaels in the Smuggler had been disturbing. The nerve of him trying to pick her up, as if she—Rhea Sinclair— were a common bar fly!

The events in the Smuggler ran through her mind until she was practically in tears. As she turned the key in the door to their apartment, the sobs broke loose.

Rhea went to bed early but lay awake. Normally the cool evening mountain air put her right to sleep. Tonight Rhea was unable to relax and her mind whirled with mind chatter. She finally got up, pulled down the shades at both windows, and closed her bedroom door. Mona wasn't home yet.

She walked over to her piano and turned on the lamp. It was the only way. She sat down and welcomed the cool touch of ivory against her fingertips as she started into Beethoven's *Moonlight*

Sonata. The steady, slow rhythm of the broken chord accompaniment sent her into a mild trance as she struck the keys that made the adagio such a haunting piece. She knew it by heart, of course.

Memories and faces appeared before her as she moved through the music. With fervor she sought to rid her head of the day's disturbances. There was a particularly annoying image of a drunken Trey Michaels hovering over her, reeking of liquor. Her heart pounded, then eased as the music soothed away the image.

Recollections of last summer intruded her thoughts as she walked. She recalled alpine picnics, the day hike up Buckskin Pass, with her hand swinging freely in the hand of Parker Sherwin. A tower of masculinity, Parker appeared taller and stronger in his Forest Service uniform. She recalled with tenderness the gentle touch as Parker placed moleskins on her blistered heels, how he had caressed her feet in the shade of an aspen grove, and smiled at her with compassionate blue eyes, his yellow hair blowing in the afternoon breeze.

Rhea held no doubts that last summer had been the happiest in her life. Before coming to Aspen for the Music Festival, she had believed her entire life comprised the piano. Years of intense study, encouraging parents, and lessons at Juilliard led to her scholarship at Aspen. Before last summer, her life had consisted of music classes, concerts and hours of excruciating practice.

But something had captivated her the moment the jet had descended onto Sardy Field that June day one year ago. The mountains overwhelmed Rhea. The air had been filled with the perfume of wildflowers that painted the green slopes, and the crisp, blue summer sky enthralled her. The sun poked its penetrating rays into her every pore, its energy rejuvenating a childhood she had stifled behind a keyboard. Rhea had felt alive for the first time in her life ... last summer.

Inspired by her new-found love of nature, she became a volunteer one day a week at the Forest Service. That's where she met Parker Sherwin, wilderness ranger in charge of seasonals and volunteers. He sent his crew off to repair gates, maintain trail heads, plant seedlings, check out campgrounds and other tasks. Rhea had grown fond of Parker, but so had the other women in the

Aspen district. Parker had those extreme good looks and build that made women swoon. He was the type of man Rhea had dreamed of, but had long given up hopes of ever meeting.

Parker had paid special attention to Rhea. It pleased her that this ideal man found her attractive. If Aspen had caused Rhea to bud, Parker Sherwin helped her blossom. Soon it was no secret that Rhea and Parker Sherwin had fallen in love.

A man of the strictest morals, Parker lived alone in government housing. He wouldn't "ruin Rhea's virtue" until they were married. Rhea had been disappointed, because she had looked forward to discovering love's fulfillment.

Summer had ended, and by mid-September the aspens had turned to gold. With the wedding one week away, a rash of fires swept through distant parts of the forest. Parker looked forward to fighting them. He loved the excitement, not to mention overtime and hazard pay. He had made light of it so often that Rhea ceased to worry about him. But, on September 23, Parker was caught in an oak brush fire. He lost his life in the attempt to save trees of little significance.

2

*T*he morning sun streaked through the windows as Rhea sat in the empty dining room of The Lucky Find. She watched two waitresses, dressed in long purple skirts and strapless tops, set condiments on the tables. Rhea glanced at her watch. Twelve minutes had passed since she had arrived—on time—for her interview. Where was the manager?

"Miss Sinclair?" A well-tanned man in his late forties, with a receding hairline, approached Rhea. The turquoise buckle on his belt pronounced his protruding gut. He extended his hand. "How's it going? My name's Olaf Cox."

"Nice to meet you, Mr. Cox." Rhea shook his hand as he took a seat across from her at the table.

"I see you brought your résumé."

Rhea handed him the typewritten page. He squinted, then pulled a pair of reading glasses out of his shirt pocket.

"Rhea ..." he commented. "What an unusual name for a beautiful young lady." The manager's eyes fell leisurely over her, then lifted to rest upon her breasts. Rhea regretted the scoop neck blouse she had chosen. If only she could change her mind and walk out right now.

"I see you have no experience working in a restaurant." Mr. Cox stroked his chin as he read over her credentials.

"None, but actually, I'm here for the piano bar job."

"Ah yes, the music student." Mr. Cox sighed. "Have you ever worked a piano bar?"

"Well, no. I taught piano lessons."

"Come with me." The manager led Rhea downstairs to the lounge. He took a seat at the bar and motioned for her to sit down at the piano. "Go ahead and play something ... anything you want."

Rhea shut her mind to the probing eyes of Mr. Cox and fell into a Guaraldi tune. Her intense training had enabled her to ignore distraction, even though she was as nervous as if it were her first audition. When she finished the piece, she looked over at him.

Mr. Cox merely stood up and nodded at her. "I'd like to use you on Thursday and Friday nights."

"How much do I get paid?" asked Rhea.

"Nine dollars an hour ... plus tips."

Nine dollars an hour was hardly enough to live on. Mona sometimes made two or three hundred dollars a night, waiting tables during the high season. But maybe there *would* be tips. Better this than those boring hours teaching piano to rich people's kids who never practiced, or even cared.

Later that day, Rhea went to the Rio Grande Trail to jog. As she stretched in preparation for her daily run, she welcomed the pleasant pull of her muscles. She drew in deep, regular breaths and soon was ready to go. She trotted to the bridge, where the trail began.

The cottonwoods shaded the jogging trail from the late afternoon sun. The rush of the river mingled with the high-pitched rapid ditty of a ruby-crowned kinglet in a nearby spruce. Rhea started out at a comfortable, unhurried pace. She cherished her daily run along the Rio Grande Trail. Last summer Parker had started her jogging. A fit body had been important to him. At first, she had protested, finding the idea of herself in jogging shorts absurd.

"Look, I'm 34 now," Parker had told her. "And in a couple of years, you'll be in *your* thirties. I want to grow up with the same lovely lady at my side—a lady as slim and healthy and beautiful as you are now."

Rhea recalled how serious he had been. Besides, he needed to stay in shape to fight forest fires. Reluctantly, Rhea started jogging with Parker. It looked easy enough. But she couldn't believe how hard it had been when she couldn't even complete half a mile. Crippled from a side stitch and gasping, she rested beside the river and watched Parker glide on down the path, having promised to pick her up on the way back.

During that first week of jogging, Rhea had almost given up. Her enthusiasm dissolved after the second day, when she was sore from toe to back. It *hurt* to run. But Parker had been patient and insisted that she continue. He made her promise to try it every day for a week. But after the week, her ankles throbbed so badly that she cried after the run, and still hadn't completed a mile.

Parker bought her an expensive pair of running shoes with treads and the support her feet needed. The difference the proper shoes made was astounding. Rhea ran her first mile that day, and she only mildly felt the pain in her ankles. She decided that since Parker had made the investment in the shoes, the least she could do was keep running.

And here she was—still running. It was more than a habit now. It was a religious experience, and she often felt Parker's spirit at her side. She could hear his voice, softly urging her on. *"Lighter steps, Rhea, lift your knees. Only half a mile further. That's my girl."*

At the Slaughterhouse Bridge Rhea turned around. She wasn't at all tired, but everything was uphill from here. By the time she finished her course, she'd have run three miles and had a good workout.

She hadn't gone far when a figure rounded the corner ahead of her. A slender, well-built man with a mustache and brown hair jogged toward her, dressed in shorts and no shirt, his breathing labored. As he approached, Rhea recognized Trey Michaels. He turned his head as they passed each other. She thought he stopped, but she didn't give him a second look.

Adrenaline flowed. Rhea sprinted uphill. After a minute, she glanced back and saw that Trey wasn't following her. In relief, she slowed, her breath rattling from the extra effort. She was upset with herself for her reaction. Why did she let the man disturb her like this?

The campus swarmed with music students the next morning when Rhea registered for the nine-week session at the Aspen

Music School. She met Jerome Hodges, headed for the music hall, carrying his French horn at his side.

"Hi, Rhea. I was hoping we'd bump into each other," he said. "How about attending the opening concert with me Friday night? The Aspen Chamber Orchestra is playing in the Tent, you know."

"I'd love to, Jerome, but I can't." Rhea explained about her new job. "But let's plan to go Saturday afternoon," she suggested. "My instructor, Caroline Bent, is going to be performing some Debussy works."

Jerome agreed to meet her at the Tent on Saturday at 3:45. "Congratulations on your new job," he said. "I have to go. I have a placement audition."

"Good luck," Rhea called after him. "See you Saturday."

The small Music School campus reminded Rhea of a garden embedded beside slopes of spruce. The rustic wooden structures scattered here and there reminded her of a quaint village with musical sounds that flowed from each dwelling. She loved to stand on the bridge that overlooked Castle Creek. The clear, bubbling water played its own soothing melody as it continued its relentless course over rocks.

Trees, ponds and grassy lawns provided a place to sit and study between meetings. Just being there, and feeling a part of nature, had inspired her enough last summer to call her back for a second session. A few people she had known last summer greeted Rhea as they walked past.

Rhea caught the next shuttle bus into town. As it wound along Castle Creek Road, she studied aspen trees as they passed and an idea took root in her mind. With sudden inspiration, she decided to step off the bus at the corner of Eighth and Hallam. When the bus stopped on the red light at Cemetery Lane, Rhea called to the driver to let her off .

The noon sun projected its rays and Rhea expected the day to be another scorcher. After the bus drove off, she crossed the busy street to the Forest Service headquarters, her purpose clear in mind. A brown, solar-designed building contained the Aspen Ranger District offices. Like many public establishments in Aspen, tourists who were used to large gaudy signs on everything had to search hard to find it. They often overlooked the head-quarters, mistaking it for a residence.

The noon whistle blew as Rhea walked up the concrete steps to the public entrance. She felt almost as though this were last summer and she was coming to meet Parker for lunch. What a comforting thought to have him safely within, perhaps—at this moment—glancing at his watch, smiling, knowing the next hour would be theirs to share.

The door stuck. Rhea had to give it an extra pull. It creaked shut behind her as she walked to the front counter, where two clerks sat. In her mind she almost heard herself ask, "Is Parker here? We're going to lunch." But, instead, she said, "Hi, Marie. Hi, Janet."

The red-haired woman, Marie, gaped at Rhea. "Well, hello, Rhea."

Janet jerked around to look. Her boyish, cropped light brown hair set off her square jaw. Both women had been with the district last summer. "Why, Rhea, what are you doing here?" Janet seemed almost shocked.

"It's wonderful to see you again." Marie was quick to recover with a smile, as if to cover up for Janet's lack of tact.

Rhea got right to the point. "I want to be a volunteer again this summer."

The two clerks looked at one another. Rhea detected skepticism in the way Janet quickly excused herself to dart into the back hallway. Marie turned to Rhea and smiled, but the telephone rang just then.

"Forest Service, Aspen District ..." Marie's voice trailed off as Rhea heard male voices laughing and talking in the hall. It was almost as if Parker could be among them. *But he wasn't.* She stared at the walls, plastered with posters of wildflowers, Woodsy Owl and Smokey the Bear.

This is a mistake. What am I doing here? Rhea wondered. *Why are they looking at me so strangely?* Remembering Janet's initial reaction, Rhea realized the only reason she had come by was to feel close to Parker. The office was the same as it was last summer. Why had she expected it not to be? But it wasn't the same. *Parker wasn't here.* An aching sadness she hadn't felt in weeks began to eat at Rhea.

"Sorry for the interruption," said Marie as she hung up the phone. "We have a new man working with the seasonals—Dick O'Neill. I think you should talk to him."

Parker's *replacement?* Oh no. Rhea hadn't realized how hard this was going to be. Her throat tightened and her eyes blurred with tears. She couldn't speak.

"Rhea, are you all right?" asked Marie.

She wasn't. Shaking her head, Rhea mumbled, "Never mind" and she left the Forest Service and started home. What a fool she had been to think she could just walk in there and pretend that things hadn't changed.

Rhea spent the afternoon practicing the piano, in preparation for her first session with the private instructor. She had an early supper and then looked for suitable sheet music for the piano bar.

Now, strains of pop hits circulated within her mind and her footsteps kept time as she slowed to a leisurely trot down the Rio Grande Trail. Parker was with her, as usual. She sensed his tall, slender form jogging at her side. She reached out her hand and could almost feel his sweaty palm squeezing hers. There was such pride in his loving blue eyes.

"*I couldn't be prouder that you've kept this up, Rhea,*" he said.

Suddenly, Rhea was aware of someone else's footsteps pounding the pavement behind her. She had to let go of his hand, but she caught the wink in Parker's eye as he broke away. She moved aside to let the other jogger pass.

"Hi," sounded a deep masculine voice. Startled, Rhea saw Trey Michaels beside her, keeping pace. Up close, she noticed his deep brown eyes and long lashes. "Been doin' this long?" he asked.

Rhea found her voice. "Oh, a while. What about yourself?"

"Well, this is new to me—this jogging thing, I mean. This is only my second day."

"Really." Rhea glanced at him. "It shows." Then she added, "But I see you're sober."

Trey started getting winded. "What's your name?" he puffed.

Rhea picked up speed. She decided the conversation had gone on long enough. "I'd rather not tell you." A second later, she broke into a sprint.

"Hey, wait up!" he called after her.

Rhea ran, paying no attention. It didn't take long to shake him. She had learned from Parker how to maintain a six-minute mile, and she could keep it up for three miles if she had to. Of course, the trail wasn't that long. When she reached the end, she slowed, then stopped at the bridge. It was growing dark as she saw Trey's huddled figure rounding the bend. He was puffing and panting.

In terrible shape, thought Rhea. She walked over to her bicycle, hopped on, and peddled home.

3

*A*t seven o'clock Thursday night, Rhea walked into The Lucky Find, wearing a pale yellow summer dress that dipped temptingly between her breasts. She noticed the dining room appeared to be busy. Tourists dominated the clientele. Downstairs in the lounge, her gaze swept over a small crowd drinking at the bar or seated at small round tables. More than a few eyes held her as she made her way to the piano.

Oh, why did I take this job? Rhea asked herself. Panic surged in her bosom as she arranged a few sheets of music before she sat down. She needed the money. She wouldn't be here except for that. Then she saw the manager, Mr. Cox, walking toward her.

"Ah, right on time." He inspected her, then nodded in approval. "You look delightful, Miss Sinclair. May I call you Rhea?"

"Of course."

"I think the crowd tonight is pretty low key. Just start out with something nice."

"I understand," said Rhea.

"Can I get you something from the bar?"

Rhea wanted a 7-Up. Mr. Cox left to get it for her and she sighed. He appeared much nicer than the morning of the interview. Perhaps this wasn't going to be so stressful after all. She shut out the curious stares and the murmur of voices, then fell into a blues tune. She was aware of Mr. Cox setting the glass of 7-Up on top of the piano. He departed with a wink.

A smattering of applause followed the first couple of numbers, but then it tapered off as the patrons grew accustomed to the musical background. A sip of her 7-Up revealed a touch of brandy. Rhea let it set until the ice melted. She kept waiting for someone to come around and deposit a dollar or two.

Rhea played for an hour and then took a break. So far, no one had come around to even talk to her. Where were all those tips? She went to the restroom to replenish her lipstick. One of the waitresses emerged from a stall and came over to wash her hands.

"Hey, you're good," the waitress told Rhea.

"Thanks."

The waitress, thin, with dark braids, had on too much eye makeup. "It's nice having some decent music for a change." She smiled. "I'm Beth."

Rhea introduced herself, then asked, "Do you like working here?"

"It's okay," said Beth. "I've been here six months. I make good money during season. You should too, if you keep on playing that good." Rhea thought Beth sounded a little tipsy. "Of course, you gotta put up with the Old Cocksucker."

"You mean ... Mr. Cox?"

"The one and only." Beth laughed, then wiped her hands with a brown paper towel. "But you'll get used to it. We all had to."

Rhea wasn't certain she knew what Beth meant. She applied her lipstick as the waitress left.

"See ya around," Beth called.

Rhea grabbed a towel to wipe the corner of her mouth. Brown paper towel smell mingled with detergent soap and general bathroom odor. She crumpled the towel and tossed it, then went back into the dim lounge. She couldn't help smiling when she saw the manager with his gut hanging out. *Mr. Cocksucker, indeed.* She wondered if he knew what his waitresses called him.

After a while she played a recent Broadway tune for a change of pace. When she looked up, there stood Jerome Hodges. He seemed a little out of place, but it was a relief to see a familiar face. Rhea finished the piece, then smiled at him.

"Jerome, what a pleasant surprise."

"I had to come down and hear you play," he said. "How's it going?"

Rhea shrugged.

"That bad, huh?"

Rhea leaned over and whispered, "I haven't made a single tip in two hours."

Jerome looked around at the patrons and shrugged. "It's a dive. What did you expect?"

"Well ..."

Mr. Cox appeared as if out of nowhere. "Is this man harassing you, Rhea?"

Jerome scrunched up his thick face beneath the glasses. "I beg your pardon."

"Why, no, Mr. Cox," Rhea insisted. "This is a friend of mine."

The manager eyed Jerome's pulpy build, amused. "A music student, no doubt," he smirked.

"What's that supposed to mean?" Rhea couldn't help feeling defensive.

The manager ignored her. "What do you play? No, let me guess." Mr. Cox chuckled sarcastically. "I know ... the piccolo."

If Jerome was insulted, he didn't show it. He nodded, his squinty eyes moving from Rhea to Mr. Cox and back to Rhea. He knew better than to provoke a quarrel, Rhea knew. She had often admired Jerome for his ability to remain calm. Jerome wasn't even going to give Mr. Cox the satisfaction of taunting him further. But before Rhea could explain to her boss that Jerome Hodges was a master French hornist, Mr. Cox got called away by the bartender.

"Go on, play some more," urged Jerome. He pulled out his wallet. "I'll get those tips started for you."

About to protest, Rhea sighed. She looked up as a young couple appeared and made a request. The young man dropped a crumpled bill onto the piano. Fortunately, Rhea knew the tune and—after tinkering with it a moment—was able to improvise and use her knowledge of sequence. The piece was rough, but the couple loved it and applauded.

By eleven-thirty Rhea had played several requests and her tips had increased. Jerome didn't stay. She recalled waving at him as he left. Things had picked up and Mr. Cox watched, with a satisfied smile, from his watchtower at the corner of the bar.

Rhea decided to wind down with a lethargic jazz interpretation when Mona walked in. She had apparently just gotten off work at Gustav's. Mona ordered a drink from the bar and came over to the piano.

Just then, Mr. Cox came up from behind Rhea. "You look beat," he said. "Why don't you knock off early?" He placed his hot hands on her shoulders.

Rhea flinched and struck a wrong chord, but continued playing. She didn't like his touch. Just who did he think he was? She reached for her tip money, then stood up, breaking his grip.

"What's the matter, doll?"

She could smell alcohol on his breath. "Actually, I am exhausted," she said. "I think I *will* go home." She gathered up her music.

"Stay and have a drink first," said Mr. Cox. The look in his bloodshot eyes reminded Rhea of Beth's conversation in the restroom. Was Mr. Cox trying to come onto her? Did he try to make it with all of his help? She shuddered.

Mona approached, drink in hand. "So how did the first night go?"

Rhea sighed and gave Mona a pleading look. Mona noticed Mr. Cox and seemed to comprehend in an instant. Mona guzzled half her drink, then thrust the glass into the manager's hand.

"Here, hold this. We'll be right back." Mona winked, then ushered Rhea toward the restrooms. When they thought Mr. Cox was no longer watching, Mona led Rhea upstairs and out of the restaurant.

"Bye!" Beth called after them.

Rhea giggled in relief once they were outside. "You saved my life."

"Oh, you'd have gotten out of that one yourself," said Mona. "I know the type. *Dirty old man!*"

Tired, Rhea went straight to bed as soon as they got home. She had a dream that she was playing the piano, only it wasn't at The Lucky Find—it was either at a school, or an orphanage, in some town she didn't know. A swarm of children surrounded her when, suddenly, a telephone rang and a voice called out, "Mrs.

Sherwin ... Mrs. Sherwin, the telephone is for you."

Startled, Rhea stopped in the middle of a tune. She realized the telephone was for her. She realized *she* was Mrs. Sherwin— Parker's wife! How had it happened? How had she suddenly become a married woman? She reached for the phone and said hello.

"Darling." It was Parker's voice. But how could it be?

"Parker? Is it really you?"

"Yes, beloved. And I'm waiting for you. Here we are married and we haven't even spent the night together yet."

It no longer mattered how the wedding had taken place. Parker was alive! Rhea hung up the phone in complete ecstasy. She'd go to him, yes ... she could hardly wait. But she found herself surrounded by crying children, who all needed to be comforted before she could get away. By then, it might be too late ... the thought caused Rhea to wake up with a start.

"You're not concentrating," scolded Ms. Bent.

With a sigh, Rhea dropped her hands. Then she started again at the top of the Rondo. She played three measures when her instructor, Ms. Caroline Bent, interrupted her.

"My dear, your mind is simply not on it."

"I'm sorry. You're right," said Rhea. "I just can't seem to concentrate today."

Ms. Bent, in her mid-fifties, sat tall with perfect posture on a wrought iron stool next to the piano bench. Her straight gray hair had been pulled tightly into a roll behind her head. Her heavy eyeshadow reminded Rhea of a ballet instructor. Although Ms. Bent wore a strict face most of the time, she now smiled warmly at Rhea, her bright red lipstick prominent. "My dear, what is troubling you?"

Rhea could think of two excuses—working late last night, and her miserable dream—but they seemed frivolous in the presence of someone as distinguished as the renowned Caroline Bent. She had no excuse for her mind wandering.

"You young ladies ... I see it all the time," Ms. Bent chided. "I'd say your trouble is undoubtedly a man. Am I right?"

Astounded by the teacher's insight, Rhea wondered how Ms. Bent could know that Parker had been on her mind. "It's not what you think," she said.

"We must get Mr. Whoever-He-Is off your mind," chided Ms. Bent. "Now, tell me his name."

"Who?"

"Why, your boyfriend, my dear. The one interfering with your playing. It will help, believe me."

Rhea felt her cheeks turn red. Tears clouded her vision. She realized this must be one of Ms. Bent's tactics for getting her to concentrate on her music, but Rhea felt ridiculous.

"Ms. Bent, I don't have a boyfriend."

"Come, come, a girl as pretty as you are?"

A sob broke loose and Rhea hated herself, but she couldn't bear to have Ms. Bent go on riding her. The next thing she knew, she had spilled the whole story out to her instructor, who listened and supplied her with tissues.

"Poor dear. Of course you have every reason to be upset." Ms. Bent handed her one more tissue to blow her nose. "But you know, certainly by now, that life goes on."

Rhea nodded, knowing it was what Ms. Bent expected of her.

"Now, I want you to go back to the music." Ms. Bent resumed her strict air and tapped the arm of her chair with a pencil. Then she hummed the rapid first bars of the Rondo, emphasizing the staccato notes as Rhea placed her hands on the keyboard.

With her emotions swept aside, Rhea returned to her lesson. At the end of the hour, the instructor seemed satisfied with her progress. Nothing more was said of Parker.

"I am scheduling you for a Tuesday concert," Ms. Bent announced while Rhea put her music away. "How about one week from next Tuesday? At noon, at the theater on Main Street."

Rhea walked across campus toward the parking lot, to wait for the next bus into town. Caroline Bent had been impressed enough to schedule her to perform in the weekly student concert. Wait till Jerome heard! A flutter of nerves, as well as exhilaration, swept through her as she began to think about what piece she could work up for the event.

As a result, she spent the rest of the afternoon practicing. Because she had to go to work again that evening, Rhea went to jog before supper. She started down the Rio Grande Trail, confident that this time she wouldn't be bothered by another encounter with Trey Michaels. Probably after his second day, he had given it up.

Somehow, the idea that he had started running because he had seen her and wanted to have an excuse to meet her flattered her. Despite his grubby appearance at first, she was attracted to the man—she couldn't help it.

"But he's just a transient. I wouldn't bother with the likes of him. You deserve better—much better."

Rhea turned to meet Parker, running next to her in spirit. "You're not jealous, are you?" she imagined herself asking him.

"Certainly you know me better than that."

An uneasiness gripped Rhea. She wanted to believe Parker was there, running beside her like before, but she realized she was running by herself. Only *her* feet pounded the blacktop along the river. She shuddered as a gnawing loneliness filled her. She forced herself to shake off the feeling.

Rhea noticed several people out jogging, biking or walking their dogs at this time. Somehow they only made Rhea feel lonelier and she tried to concentrate on her rhythm and breathing. She wished she could be alone with Parker. About halfway down the trail, somebody popped out from behind a tree and fell into pace with her.

"Hello again," said a deep voice.

Rhea gasped. "Trey!"

He laughed. "Hey, how did you know my name?"

He had surprised her and she had let her guard down. When she looked at him, his brown eyes probed hers. He seemed delighted at her confusion. She didn't know how to respond. "I ... found out," she finally said.

"Well then, I think it's only fair I find out what your name is, pretty lady."

She knew he'd just keep hounding her if she didn't tell him. "Rhea Sinclair," she said. Then she asked, "What are you doing jogging this time of day? I thought you ran at dusk."

"I could ask you the same thing." After a pause, he added, "Actually, I prefer to jog at dusk when it's cooler. But tonight, I got plans."

"Oh?" Rhea glanced at him. Sweat broke out on his flushed face. "I suppose Friday nights you reserve for going out and getting smashed with your roughneck friends."

Trey's breathing started to get heavy. "Hey, I'm not such a bad guy, really. I was going to ask you to a movie."

Rhea picked up her pace. He struggled to keep up. "Well, it just so happens I'm working tonight," she told him.

"Where do you work?"

Rhea pulled ahead of him. She wasn't about to tell him where she was working. She called back over her shoulder, "I play the piano."

"Really?" He burst forward and caught up to her, but she knew he wouldn't be able to hold it for long.

"Really."

"Well, I can meet you afterwards."

"I'd rather not." Rhea sprang ahead, then over her shoulder she shouted, "but keep on jogging!" She left him behind as a surge of adrenaline boosted her speed. So, Trey Michaels had asked her on a date. Flattered—but at the same time frightened—she knew a man like Trey could only be after one thing. She was glad she hadn't told him *where* she worked.

As she emerged from the woods and started up the hill toward home, Parker's words echoed in her mind. *"He's just a transient."* Parker certainly wouldn't approve. It wasn't that she felt guilty about dating. She just wasn't ready for any kind of relationship. She didn't want to give anyone a chance to drive a wedge between herself and Parker. And Trey Michaels frightened her. Already she found herself drawn to him and it made her feel separated from Parker, especially while jogging, which had been a sacred time for them since his death.

Trey frightened her, there was no doubt, and yet she had to admit, she enjoyed having someone beside her on the jogging trail again—someone in the flesh, who didn't enter her thoughts or probe the secret chambers of her mind.

Rhea dressed more casually for work that night. She preferred her music to be what attracted customers and not her appearance. Tonight she felt more at ease at the piano. It started out the same as last night, with no one paying much attention. But she was glad to be left alone. Thoughts sailed through her head, uninterrupted.

She fantasized an evening out on the town with Parker. Perhaps Trey's mention of asking her to a movie had prompted it. Parker had actually preferred quiet evenings at his place, and Rhea had never objected.

His house had always been tidy—like Parker himself. His bed was made whenever she came over. Dishes were stacked neatly in the sink, if not already washed and put away. He even hung up his clothes after changing. It would have been easy to be married to him. He had come to her apartment a few times. Mona had entertained quite a bit last summer and the place was usually in a shambles. Rhea had been embarrassed to have Parker see it.

But those wonderful, cozy evenings at his place ... She'd never forget the serenading crickets in the woods outside his living room window, or the cool alpine breeze caressing them, or she cuddled up on his lap. Sometimes they'd talk and make plans for the future, or Parker would read to her from his collection of classics. He loved to read, and when he had learned how little she was familiar with Thoreau, he started reading to her from *Walden*. It was soothing to lie on the rug with her head cradled in his lap, listening to the sound of his gentle voice.

Rhea's reverie was cut short as Mr. Cox leaned over the top of the piano. His bloodshot eyes swept her figure. "It's pay day, doll. You can pick up your check in my office during your break."

Uncomfortable with his presence, Rhea goofed up her number, but slid into something less difficult. "Thank you," she replied. "Does that mean I've got a steady job?"

Mr. Cox stroked his bristly chin. "I said I'd see." After a pause, he added, "Come into my office when you take your break and we'll discuss some terms."

"What terms?"

"I like you, Rhea. I want to keep you on at the piano bar. But there's your schedule to arrange. We'll talk about that in my office."

"Whatever you say." Rhea wished he'd go away. He disturbed her.

She put off her break until past ten o'clock. Then her buttocks hurt from sitting on the hard bench. She wandered over to the bar to order a soft drink. The bartender, Carl, served her a Coke with a napkin. Young—probably twenty-one—Carl wouldn't take her money.

"You work here. You don't pay," he said with a grin.

As she sipped her drink, Rhea grew aware of the customers around her. She had spent little time in bars or nightclubs. She didn't feel comfortable in this type of crowd. Mr. Cox spotted her and beckoned her over.

"Ready for that talk?" he asked.

They went through a door behind the stairway. Mr. Cox switched on the light. A dingy room with cracked concrete walls and no windows, the manager's office contained a cluttered desk and chair on one side, while a large, tattered couch took up the opposite wall. Some pornographic magazines lay scattered on the couch.

"First, let me give you your check." Mr. Cox reached for a brown envelope on his desk and fished through it. After handing her the yellow check, he closed the door and beckoned her toward the couch. "Why don't you make yourself comfortable?"

Rhea hesitated. "If you don't mind, I'll stand." After a pause, she added, "I've been sitting a long time."

Mr. Cox seemed to detect the trace of repulsion in her voice. He walked over to her. "Why are you so nervous, my dear?" He reached out and began rubbing her neck and shoulders. "This will relax those tense muscles."

Rhea backed away from the man. She had a dreadful feeling that he was going to try something. "I really should get back to the piano now."

"You can have as long a break as you want," Mr. Cox

explained and stepped closer. "And if you expect to work for me on a regular basis, you'll find that I not only allow—but *encourage*—these breaks." When he laughed, it sent a chill up Rhea's spine. Then he bent forward to kiss her.

A loud knock on the door startled them both. Rhea ducked aside.

"Excuse me, Mr. Cox." It was Carl, the bartender.

"What is it, Carl?" barked the manager.

Carl glanced at Rhea, and appeared boyish. "I'm sorry, sir. I didn't mean to interrupt anything ..."

Rhea took her chance and slipped out of the office as Carl related a problem with the cash register. She returned to the piano, upset by the episode in Mr. Cox's office. She refused to have anything to do with the disgusting man. She vowed she'd never allow herself to be alone with him again. Thank goodness, Carl had come looking for his boss just then.

Tucking her paycheck under the piano bench, Rhea composed herself and decided on what numbers she would play the rest of the night. Her hands trembled. More crowded now, the dim lounge's atmosphere appeared subdued. She livened it up with a boogie woogie and strived to shut old Mr. Cocksucker out of her mind.

Rhea's relief was short-lived, however. Before she had finished the tune, she noticed Mr. Cox, drink in hand, slithering among the shadows of the customers. She wondered how she was going to get out of there tonight. Mona wouldn't be stopping by like last night. Rhea had to get out on her own.

She played well past midnight. She stalled for time and the crowd dissipated. Only a handful of people remained. The bar would be closing soon, and there stood Mr. Cox by the stairway, waiting for her. Finally, Rhea could wait no longer. She stood up to leave. She had to go home. She was dead tired.

Carl called to her as she passed the bar. "Rhea, did you pick up your check?"

Rhea remembered she had tucked it into the piano bench. She spun around to head back to the piano when she spotted a familiar face sitting alone at a dark table. Trey Michaels sat, drinking a glass of beer. He smiled at her.

Rhea signaled a hasty greeting, then went to retrieve her paycheck, her mind in a turmoil. How long had Trey been sitting in the lounge? It seemed odd to her that he hadn't come over to say hello. Her heart fluttered at the thought of him. Her fingers trembled as she folded the paycheck and stuffed it into her backpack.

"Are you trying for overtime?" Rhea tensed up as Mr. Cox stood over her. "Because *here* you don't get overtime." His voice was hard and his alcohol breath reeked.

Rhea winced as Mr. Cox placed his hands around her waist. "There's still the little matter regarding your schedule," he said. "Let's go back into my office."

"I'm *not* going into your office." Gritting her teeth, Rhea tried to keep calm. Her body stiffened in protest as he attempted to caress her hair.

"You'll love it, doll. All my waitresses do."

"I'm *not* one of your waitresses." Rhea tried to break his grip, but he was stronger than she had imagined. Fear replaced her repulsion. "Let me go!"

"I know, I know," said Mr. Cox, "but it's necessary if you want to work for me."

That settled it. Rhea decided she wasn't coming back to work. She didn't have to put up with this kind of harassment. "Leave me alone!" This time her voice rose above the few remaining voices in the lounge. There seemed to be no choice but to make a scene.

Suddenly, Mr. Cox slipped back and Rhea heard the smack as a fist hit a jaw. She saw Trey Michaels beside her, and Mr. Cox crouched on the floor, his hands over his face.

Trey stepped back and rubbed his fist. He turned to Rhea. "Are you all right?"

Rhea nodded at him. Mr. Cox groaned, but seemed unhurt. Drunk, he lost his balance trying to get up. Carl and some others gathered around.

"Want me to call the cops, boss?"

Oh no, thought Rhea, *not the police.*

"There's more where that came from, if he harasses this lady ever again," Trey told them.

To Rhea's relief, Mr. Cox shook his head and brushed himself off as he staggered to his feet. He shot a hateful glare at Trey.

"Beat it!" yelled Mr. Cox. "You too," he told Rhea. "And ... you're fired!"

Trey wrapped an arm around Rhea and together they left. They hastened up the stairs and out into the cool night air.

"Are you sure you're all right?" Trey asked again, his deep voice gentler. He let go of her as they stood on the sidewalk outside.

"I guess so." Embarrassed, she stared down at her feet. "I've never been fired before."

Trey laughed. "You'll find another job. A lady that plays a mean piano ought to be able to write her own ticket." Then he asked, "Can I drive you home?"

Rhea shivered in the night air. As grateful as she was to Trey for rescuing her from Mr. Cox, she didn't know whether to trust him. "It's not far. I can walk."

"Come on." He drew her close and his warmth surged through her. She didn't draw away. Together, they walked in the direction of the street. Trey helped her into his pickup truck, which smelled of hay and leather. He tossed a pair of ragged jeans into the back seat, then started up the engine.

"Where to?" asked Trey.

Rhea gave him her address and Trey shifted into gear, then pulled out from the curb. She wanted to say something, *anything*. Small talk was certainly better than this silence. When he pulled up in front of her apartment building, the porch light beckoned in the darkness.

"Thanks for the ride," said Rhea. The door stuck when she tried to open it.

"Wait, I'll get it." Trey jumped out of the truck and opened the door from the outside. Then he extended his arm to help her down. At the touch of his hand in hers, Rhea felt a rush of energy. He lifted her down and, for a brief moment, she felt his strength as he held her.

"Thank you," she told him.

His face inches from hers, he asked, "For what?"

A wave of desire made Rhea catch her breath. Uncontrollable thoughts awoke in her mind. What would it be like, she wondered, to feel his face pressed against hers? His lips touching hers in full force? Overwhelmed by her attraction to him, she didn't want him to walk her to the door, but he did just that.

"Maybe I shouldn't thank you," she added.

"Why?"

"Well, after all, I did lose my job."

"And you're sorry?" They stood under the porch light and she could see his face clearly.

"I needed the job," she said. Her heart pounded.

"I could see that." A jeering edge crept into his voice.

Rhea fumbled through her pack, looking for her apartment keys. "You think I was leading him on?"

Trey sighed. "What do you suppose would have happened if I hadn't come over and socked him?"

"Nothing," she lied. Rhea didn't want to talk about it any more.

Trey moved closer. The next thing she knew, he clutched her. He kissed her hard on the mouth and his lips overcame her own. Taken by surprise, Rhea could not resist. Stormy feelings surfaced and her whole body swam in a frenzy, in one long, delicious moment.

When he released her, she stood there, dazed. He backed away, then let go of her hand. She watched him return to his truck. "Good night," he called before he swung in.

She couldn't find her voice in time to reply, until the truck was halfway down the block.

4

*T*he next morning Rhea slept late. She fixed a late breakfast and sat down to eat at the kitchen table. Mona wandered in, still in her bathrobe.

"Do we have any coffee left?" asked Mona. She pulled a mug from the dish rack and poured herself a cup.

"I didn't hear you come in last night," said Rhea.

Mona sat down. "It was late. How did work go for you last night? Is it any better?"

Rhea explained all that had happened with Mr. Cox and how Trey Michaels had shown up and slugged the manager. "And now I'm out of a job," she added.

"You ought to sue the S.O.B. for sexual harassment," cried Mona.

Rhea sighed. "It's not worth the bother."

Mona stared at her. "So ... Trey Michaels brought you home last night. Well, well, well."

"Don't start, Mona. Nothing happened."

"I wonder why he was hanging around The Lucky Find." Mona took a sip of coffee. "That doesn't seem to be the kind of place a guy like that would hang out at." She got up to get some creamer out of the refrigerator. "He must have heard you were playing there."

Rhea took a bite of her toast. "Well, I'm not going back."

Mona didn't give up. "Rhea, I think you're stuck on this guy."

"You're wrong."

"Then why did he come between you and your boss? It must have bothered him seeing you in that predicament. And he obviously cared enough to intervene. By the way, where did you two meet?"

"Mona ... do we have to talk about Trey?"

Mona sat down again. "I just want to know the facts."

Rhea sighed. "If you must know, we've seen each other down by the river ... jogging."

"*Oh* ... jogging."

"Just jogging on the Rio Grande." Rhea tried to sound casual.

"Well, I'll tell you what I know about Trey Michaels," said Mona. "It's not much, but I know he's working over at the Nickelson Creek Ranch."

"I know, you told me that already," said Rhea.

"Oh, I did. That's right, you can't stand cowboys."

Rhea made no comment.

"But you've got to admit," said Mona, "Trey isn't bad-looking."

Rhea remembered last night and the kiss under the porch light. She almost sighed, but she didn't want Mona to know anything about that. She'd never hear the end of it. "Actually, you're right. Trey is very good-looking."

Mona snorted. "*Good-looking?* That man is one hunk!"

"Mona, you were rude to him that night in the bar," Rhea reminded her roommate.

"I was just testing you. You're hot for him, Rhea Sinclair, and don't you deny it."

Rhea knew she couldn't put one over on Mona, but she still held her ground. "Even if I am, it can't work. We're too different, he and I. I'll bet he can't stand classical music. We don't have a thing in common."

"Not even jogging?"

"That doesn't count."

"I think you should go out with him."

Rhea drank some coffee. "I'm not ready to date anyone."

"That's what you've been saying all winter," Mona grumbled. "When are you going to get over Parker, for heaven's sake?"

"Probably never." Annoyed, Rhea carried her dishes to the sink. She escaped into her bedroom and shut the door. There, she picked up her most treasured picture of Parker and brushed her lips against the cold glass. Then she held the frame to her breast as hot tears seeped from her eyes. Parker's brother, a professional photographer, had taken the picture of Parker two summers ago, a year before Rhea had met him, when the two brothers had gone on a fishing trip together. She loved how his brother had captured him so casually beside a mountain lake, as if his smile had been aimed at the future, just for her.

She closed her eyes and remembered what it had felt like to be close to Parker. His lips, his touch, had always been tender and loving. She remembered the first time he had kissed her, after the staff picnic at the district ranger's house. Because she was the newcomer around the government employees, Rhea had felt shy. The day had been kind of gloomy and overcast. It had been the day she came to realize how strong her feelings were for Parker.

Up till that party, they had stayed strictly on a business relationship. She had remained unusually quiet at the picnic, watching the other women on the staff attempt to win Parker's approval. Their flirting had made Rhea feel diminished, even spinsterish. She almost didn't stay.

Then Parker found her, sulking in a corner at the ranger's house, after the party had moved indoors to get out of the rain. He told her he didn't like crowds either and suggested they slip out for a walk together in the woods, once the rain let up. Rhea's life changed that day.

They strolled across the Forest Service property, hand in hand. It didn't matter that the woods was only a small section of trees through which they could walk to get to Parker's house. Nor did they notice the traffic noises a block away, where Highway 82 entered Aspen's city limits. He asked her things about herself, where she was from, where she had gone to school. Then he told her about himself. They had come to Aspen from opposite directions, Parker from California, Rhea from the Midwest.

Neither cared to return to the party, even though it was still early. They sat in the woods and talked, the fresh smell of wet leaves heavy in the air. Rhea's pants got soaked from sitting on the moist ground. Parker pointed to a woodpecker he had spotted high in the trees and identified it as a yellow-bellied sapsucker.

"It's crazy, don't you think?" Parker smiled at her as they sat

next to each other on the wet ground, his blue eyes bright. "Here
you and I have been working side by side for two weeks. You didn't
notice, but I've been waiting for an opportunity like this."

Rhea wanted to admit that yes, she *had* noticed. She wanted
to confess her true feelings, but she hadn't wanted Parker to put
her in the same category as the other adoring females who made
fools of themselves.

Then he had kissed her. Sitting close together on the wet
earth, she had allowed a fragile, yet tender kiss. Rhea had been in
heaven. She snuggled up to him and welcomed the long arms that
draped her. The deeper, second kiss caused them to slide back
onto the grass. Afterwards he laughed and pulled her up.

"You must be chilled," said Parker. "Come on, I'll take you to
my house."

The abrupt ending had been Rhea's first hint that Parker
was no ordinary man. If sex had been all he wanted, plenty of
opportunities existed on the staff alone. There were times later in
their courtship when she had wanted to make love, but he had
been the one to stop before anything got started.

Now Rhea wished she had pushed harder. She had longed for
it, but respected Parker's wishes and withheld the fulfillment of
her desires. She didn't realize the dream they both had built
would never unfold.

At four o'clock that afternoon, Rhea stood outside the huge
white Music Tent in Aspen's west end. She searched the faces of
concert goers, then spotted Jerome Hodges at the refreshment
stand. Hard to miss, she went over to greet him.

"Hi, Rhea." He paid for two lemonades and handed her one.
"Been waiting long? I hope not."

"No, I just got here."

"Say, why aren't you wearing glasses?"

"Jerome, I've had contacts since last summer."

"Really?" He drank his lemonade. "Well, you look fine."

It was just like Jerome not to notice till now, Rhea thought.
"Shall we go in now? We'll be lucky to find a seat," she said.

The tent was always well occupied for weekend concerts, but

Rhea and Jerome managed to find seats close to the stage. The day was partly sunny with a slight breeze. When the wind blew, the tent walls flapped and seemed as though it might rise, like a hot air balloon.

Jerome told about his classes and asked her about hers. Rhea explained about the student concert one week from Tuesday. Excited for her, Jerome said he'd come, and they discussed some works she could perform.

"I thought I'd play something contemporary for a change," said Rhea.

Jerome's face scrunched into a sourball. "Stick with the old-timers," he said. "That's what you do best."

"But everyone is up on more modern compositions these days."

"Yes, but no one brings out the feelings like you do. Stick to Mozart."

Rhea sighed. Jerome would naturally feel that way, being a French hornist. She turned her attention to the stage, where the first performers on the program walked out. The audience applauded.

Caroline Bent was second on the program. This was what Rhea had been waiting for. She felt a glow of pride at being a student of the woman as she applauded Ms. Bent's entrance. Dressed in a violet silk formal, Ms. Bent sat at the piano as straight as a pin. Looking as composed as a ballerina, the master pianist sent Rhea into a dream world that encompassed Claude Debussy and the enthralling sounds of mystery and beauty that he had conjured out of the piano.

Rhea was familiar with just about everything the man had composed. Her passion for him had made her a rather accomplished performer of his major piano works. Watching Ms. Bent, Rhea could anticipate her every move, feeling the chords and the ripples. She was intrigued at how her instructor interpreted them in a unique way, never hesitating. The last number, *La Cathedrale engloutie*, was too much for Rhea to bear. Its haunting, bell-like colors drew her away from the reality of the concert into the austere depths of her imagination until tears filled her eyes.

At the last sustained chord of Ms. Bent's rendition, Rhea sobbed as the audience filled the tent with their resounding applause. She sniffed with embarrassment as Jerome studied her curiously.

"Isn't she wonderful?" Rhea asked over the clapping.

"Are you okay?" Jerome asked.

"Of course." Rhea dabbed at her eyes.

The intermission followed and Jerome insisted they go outside for some fresh air. "How about another lemonade?" he asked. Rhea declined, but Jerome bought one for himself. "By the way," he said, "a bunch of us are getting together the Fourth of July weekend for a campout. Are you interested in joining us?"

Camping was one thing Rhea had done little of—Parker had promised to take her sometime. "Who's going?" she asked.

"A bunch of us from the Music School. Myself, Oliver Knight, JoAnn Bartelli ... some others."

Rhea didn't know any of those people well. They were mostly friends of Jerome. It didn't sound like much fun. "I don't know."

"We're planning on hiring a guide and going up to Snowmass Lake on horseback."

Rhea had to laugh, trying to picture herself on a horse. "No thanks, Jerome."

"Don't turn down this fantastic opportunity before you've thought about it first," he said. "Let me find out more about it and then you can decide."

Rhea agreed to that, at least. Jerome was so good-hearted and he was tactful enough not to pry about why she had been crying. Jerome seemed to understand without being told.

Rhea practiced the piano almost all day on Sunday. She played some Debussy and was disappointed at how inferior it sounded after listening to Caroline Bent's concert. The phone rang as she was getting something to eat. Since her parents were in the habit of calling on Sundays, she hurried to answer it. She had been toying with the idea of calling them and asking for some money to tie her over until she could find another part-time job.

"Rhea?" The voice that responded to her greeting was a man's.

"Yes?" For a fearful moment she thought it might be Mr. Cox calling her back to her job.

"Are you free tonight?"

"Who is this?" But even as she asked, Rhea realized who was calling—Trey Michaels.

He laughed. "It's me, the fella who saved a damsel in distress at The Lucky Find the other night."

Rhea relaxed and grew excited at the same time. "Oh, hello, Trey. What did you want?"

"I was wonderin' if you were free tonight. Actually, I tried getting hold of you yesterday, but there was no answer." He paused. Rhea didn't feel like explaining that she had been at the concert with Jerome. "So, what do you say? Are you up to it?"

Rhea drew in a breath. Her fingers began twisting the telephone cord. An urgency she didn't understand was rising within her. She wanted to take a chance. He had been there for her when she needed him. But he still scared her. "I'd like to, Trey, but ... I can't."

"Well, why not?"

"I have to ... practice the piano."

It was a lousy excuse and Trey knew it. "What's the real reason?"

Rhea couldn't think of another way out. "I ... wouldn't feel right about it."

"Oh." Trey was silent a moment. "There's another man in your life. I should have known." He sounded almost defeated.

Rhea perked up. "That's it," she told him. "I wouldn't want to hurt his feelings, and if I went out with you ..."

"Well, he doesn't have to know," Trey interrupted. "Just don't tell him." There was a short silence, then he asked, "What's wrong? Are you engaged to the guy or something?"

It was hitting too close to home. Rhea felt a lump in her throat and swallowed. "I was," she said in a small voice.

"But you're not anymore? That means there's hope," said Trey. "So what's wrong with just going out one night with a friend? I don't care if you have your designs on someone else. I just want to talk and have a good time."

Rhea sighed. "Trey, I can't start seeing you. Please understand."

Trey lingered a moment, then said, "Well, if you've already got a man, okay. But I sure wouldn't have thought it after the other night."

"What are you talking about?"

"You wanted me," he said. "Just as much as I wanted you. Those sweet lips of yours, honeybabe." He fell into the Texas drawl again. "Those lips weren't lyin'."

Rhea had heard enough. She slammed the phone down. Her suspicions had been right—he was only after one thing. And to think she had almost accepted a date with him!

5

*R*hea ran at dusk. A glimmer of excitement prompted her as she started down the trail. What a perfect time to jog. Sunset layers of orange streaked the sky and the air felt cool and fresh. Rhea felt alive and strong as the rush of blood churned throughout her body. After a hard day's practice at the piano, it was good to run, to feel alive in more than just head and hands.

Other joggers passed her, and each time she saw a male figure her heart would flutter as she thought of Trey Michaels. It would be just like Trey to intercept her again and try to convince her to go somewhere with him.

"You're in good form tonight, Rhea. What's the rush? Why don't you slow down?"

Rhea looked around and found Parker running beside her. She was a bit surprised because her mind had been focused on Trey. "I'm not going too fast, am I?"

"Yes, you are. What's your hurry?"

"No hurry." What was this—the third degree? Resentment began to build, but as she turned to him and met his loving smile, the cold feeling dissolved. How she wanted to reach out and squeeze his hand, stop running and fall into his arms. But this wasn't real. She couldn't feel his warm hand in hers. Suddenly she felt ashamed without knowing why. Her pace slackened.

"That's better," said Parker. *"I was afraid you wanted to run away from me."*

"No! Why would you think that?"

Another male jogger rounded the curve ahead and Rhea tensed up. It wasn't Trey. She relaxed.

"Don't worry," said Parker after a moment. *"Our pal is not on*

the trail tonight."

Rhea wished Parker wasn't running with her now. With just a thought she could make him vanish. The way Parker referred to Trey as "our pal" annoyed her.

"That is *what you were afraid of?"* Parker continued.

Rhea couldn't deny it when her feelings were constantly exposed to him like this. "I hoped we might see him," she admitted. "I was rather mean to him on the phone earlier and I wanted to apologize."

"He called you up? That transient?"

"Parker, don't call him that."

"But I don't trust him, Rhea. And you shouldn't either." When she didn't respond, he said, *"You like him, don't you?"* There was a grudge in Parker's voice.

"Let's not discuss Trey Michaels," Rhea pleaded. "I just want to run."

"Okay. We'll just run."

In the twilight Rhea ran home. The apartment was dark. Mona was at work. She wasn't sure if it was relief or disappointment that filled her. Suddenly Rhea felt an aching loneliness. Jogging had not given her what she needed tonight. She and Parker had argued—to a certain extent—and it left an empty pain in the pit of her stomach.

Stepping out onto the balcony, Rhea stood in the cool mountain air and listened to the night sounds. Only a block away, Main Street was in full swing. Aspen's night life was vibrant and at its peak. A man and a woman walked by on their way to a downtown night spot. The lights just went out in the neighbor's Victorian. The moon, bright and almost full, silhouetted Smuggler Mountain to the east.

Rhea wondered if Trey was out on the town. Was he part of the night crowd, drinking beer in some bar where loud country music blared? Had he found some other girl who would go out with him? A guy as attractive and carefree as Trey undoubtedly had no trouble finding someone to spend the night with—he was obviously that kind of guy.

How different he was from Parker, who had been serious and

settled in his habits and philosophies. Parker had been an educated man with a future and an appreciation for Rhea's talent and her mind. That was the kind of man Rhea had wanted and that is what she had found. No one had come close before she met Parker, nor after he was gone.

And Trey was so far from comparison, it was ridiculous. Yet the memory of his kiss under the porch light still came back to haunt Rhea in all of its ecstasy. She shivered in the cold and wandered back inside the apartment. Maybe she had done it after all. Trey had finally gotten the message. She had best forget that magical moment they had shared because it wasn't going to happen again. With despair she realized Trey may never call her again.

The next three nights when Rhea jogged there was no sign of Trey. She decided he must have given up running and she was sorry. But she knew she'd get over the disappointment. Why she cared one way or another puzzled her. Even with Parker's spirit at her side, jogging was turning into a lonely sport. She began to resent Parker's intrusion on her thoughts. A tension developed between the two of them and Rhea preferred to be left alone while she ran. Parker stayed with her, but ran silently, refusing to go away.

Thursday came and while Rhea had been busy with her classes and practice, she still did not have a job. It was nearing the end of the month and she knew Mona expected her portion of the rent money. Rhea strolled out toward Main Street late in the afternoon. She wanted to buy an *Aspen Times* to see what job possibilities were in the classified ads.

When she arrived in front of the old historic newspaper office, a crowd had gathered. Obviously the paper was not out yet. A cardboard sign hung over the door that said TODAY'S PAPER OUT AT 4:15.

Tourists were infiltrating the town. Campers and motorhomes rolled by on their way off Independence Pass. She recognized other music students, many carrying their instruments in cases. Then she saw Jerome Hodges crossing the intersection and she hurried over to intercept him.

"Hey, I'm glad I ran into you," said Jerome. "Our trip for next weekend is on." He set his French horn down on the sidewalk and wiped his pale sweaty forehead. "The Lawrences are going. They're sort of paying for the trip—you know, renting the horses and so on. I told them you were thinking about coming along. They want you to join us."

The Lawrences, Rhea knew, were Professor Arthur Lawrence and his wife Elizabeth, two faculty members from Music Associates of Aspen. Rhea had forgotten about Jerome's proposed trip. She was acquainted with the Lawrences, of course, and they were nice people. After a depressing week, the prospect of getting away for a weekend suddenly appealed to her. She found out they were planning to leave the following Friday afternoon.

"We'll return on Sunday," explained Jerome. "All you need to bring is a sleeping bag and a change of clothes."

"What about food?" asked Rhea.

Jerome shrugged. "The Lawrences are buying the food." He cocked his head. "Does this mean you'll go?"

It sounded too good to be true. Rhea said she'd go. Jerome promised to call her before next week about where to meet, then picked up his horn and continued on his way.

Mozart's *Sonata in A Minor, K. 310* became Rhea's obsession over the weekend as she prepared for the student concert. She planned to play the first movement. It was a rapid, tiring piece to perform. She wore herself out after each one-hour sitting and had to take several breaks during her practice sessions. But she stuck to it. It would have been easier, perhaps, to work up something she already knew and felt comfortable with, but Debussy or Ravel were too emotional for her. Rhea strove to keep a clear head with so many feelings poking at her these days. With Mozart she felt disciplined and in control.

Late Tuesday morning Rhea walked downtown toward the courthouse, confident and excited. She thrived on preparing for concerts, which gave her a high. She only wished she had someone special to play for. In her younger years it had been her parents.

How proud they would look, seated in the audience at her recitals. Last summer it had been Parker for whom she had poured out her heart through her music. Her overpowering love for him had filled her soul with a rapture she had never known. She had reached that point in her career where her inner essence took over her playing and she no longer feared wrong notes or slips. The music had taken over and she was grateful to Parker for giving her that.

But today she wouldn't have his encouraging smile out in the audience. *He'll still be there if I want him to be*, Rhea told herself as she crossed Main Street at Hunter. She would still play for Parker. She knew he heard her music and was listening with the same devoted appreciation as when he had been alive.

As she passed St. Mary's Church with its brick walls and stained glass cross, a shiver of uncertainty passed through Rhea —her first wave of nerves. How could she possibly play Mozart for all those people? She sighed. They were, after all, only the locals of the town, gathered on their lunch hour to hear free classical music. Anybody could attend. Quite likely higher-ups from M.A.A. would be there to critique their protégés. Ms. Bent most certainly would be there with her critical ear.

I'll be fine, really, Rhea told herself as she entered the building. Some students she knew from the Music Festival greeted her and the sudden panic slipped away as she joined the other performers.

"Hi, Rhea." Jerome Hodges found her backstage. "Are you nervous?"

"You're not supposed to ask her that," snickered Marla Wentworth, standing next to them. She was the first music student to perform. "Look at *me*, I'm shaking like a leaf."

"Jerome, I'm glad you came," said Rhea.

"Well, I'm afraid I can't stay for it all," he said. "I may not get to hear you play."

"Jerome, did you go to Calligraphy yesterday?" Marla asked.

Their conversation drifted away as Rhea wandered out into the lobby for a drink of water. People sauntered into the auditorium. They were all ages, dressed mostly in shorts and jeans. Tourists stood out in their colorful summer wardrobes. Rhea returned backstage and after a while things grew quiet and the stage manager summoned Marla.

She performed a modern-day composition on the piano that made Rhea glad Jerome had talked her out of choosing something contemporary. If Marla made any mistakes, no one but the composer and herself could know it. A clatter of applause followed Marla backstage, then died down. A rustle of movement and coughing signified a restless audience as the second performer, Bruce Fischer, a trombonist, and his accompanist walked out on stage.

Rhea peeked out the curtain to see how large an audience there was today. The auditorium was large, so it made the group of sixty or so people gathered at the front seem like only a handful. Several rows had filled up, though, she noticed. A few people sat toward the back, eating their lunches out of brown paper sacks.

Bruce's performance began as Rhea scanned the faces for Ms. Bent or Jerome. She stopped short when her eyes fell on somebody in the front row. "I don't believe it," she whispered aloud.

"What is it?" Marla's voice whispered into her ear.

Trey Michaels sat in the very front row of the audience. Rhea had to smile at how out of place he looked just now, sitting there completely bored with the trombone solo.

With all her practicing she had tucked Trey into the back of her mind, especially since he had not called again or met her jogging down by the river. She had been unable to forget Trey, but seeing him here today was a total surprise. It was the last place she expected to find him. She decided that after the concert she would make a point to linger outside in the lobby. Maybe he'd stop and talk with her a few moments. *Why else would he have come?* she wondered.

"Rhea, you're next," called the stage manager as the clapping signified the end of Bruce's solo. Rhea took a couple of deep breaths as her blood surged and she grew warm and excited. In a minute she would be out on that stage, the center of attention.

"I'm ready," she replied.

"You'll do great," Marla told her.

Bruce and his accompanist appeared backstage then. That

was Rhea's cue. She stepped out and walked over to the grand piano on center stage as a soft ripple of applause greeted her entrance. Glancing over at Trey in the front row, she saw his look of admiration and smiled at him. He grinned in return and Rhea was suddenly overcome with inspiration. Trey sat straight and erect in his seat.

Rhea sat down and gave herself a few seconds to prepare her frame of mind. Then she began to play the sonata. The moment she plunged into it, Rhea knew it was happening just the way she had planned. The sharp staccato chords chopped along at a fast clip, steady and blatant. The melody was strong with the running sixteenths clear and even. She felt power in her fingers. After the nine or ten minutes it took to get through the repeats and the closing climax, Rhea's muscles ached from the strain. But she didn't let up. There was no turning back until that final crescendo and the three closing chords.

Had she been at home Rhea would have slumped against her keyboard after such an exhausting execution. Instead she caught herself and rose from the bench to face the audience as the theater filled with thunderous applause. Rhea was astounded that such a small gathering of concert goers could create such a noise—and for *her!* The clapping continued, lasting at least twice as long as that of Marla's or Bruce's performances. Rhea took her bow, then retreated quickly backstage. Her comrades were applauding and she didn't quite know what to do.

"You were fantastic, Rhea," someone called out.

"Absolutely marvelous," added Marla.

"Go on out and take another bow," prompted the stage manager.

Rhea was reluctant. After all, this was only a student weekly concert, not Carnegie Hall. The applause waned and she hesitated. "No, it's Mitsuko's turn." She beckoned to the young Japanese violinist.

The short Oriental girl bowed her head. "You expect me to go on after that?"

Rhea blushed. Mitsuko was a child prodigy at 16. "Break a leg," said Rhea.

"Beg a pardon?"

Mitsuko's accompanist twittered as he urged the soloist on stage. "It's only an American expression," he explained.

Rhea slipped into the lobby for another drink of water. Jerome came out of the auditorium just then. "Hey, that was high class," he congratulated her. "Am I glad I stayed."

"Thank you, Jerome."

"Too bad Ms. Bent wasn't here," he said.

"Oh, she wasn't?" Rhea felt disappointed.

"Don't worry. She'll hear about it." Jerome had to leave, but he reminded her once again of where and when they would be meeting the Lawrences that Friday for the campout. Rhea promised to be there.

The sonata had drained Rhea, but she wanted to hear Mitsuko's violin playing, so she quietly slipped into the auditorium and stood at the back to watch. The Japanese girl was truly a wonder, a fitting end to the day's concert.

Then Rhea noticed that Trey was no longer seated in the front row. She scanned the audience, but Trey was not among them. He had vanished from the crowd. She waited outside the theater as all the people exited, but there was no sign of Trey. Apparently he had left the concert immediately after her performance.

Rhea's spirits sank in a heap. The least he could have done was hang around and say hello. As she wandered home, she realized it was just too late. *She* had been the one to turn *him* down, after all. Hadn't she made it clear to him that she didn't want to date him? She had come right out and told him she didn't want to start seeing him. Now she was sure he had given up on her and there was nothing she could do about it.

So let it be. Let the dirtbag cowboy stick with his own kind, she told herself. He was the last thing she needed to complicate her life. And hadn't he already interfered enough with Parker?

Crossing to the corner where the church stood, Rhea lingered a few moments to admire the flowers along the black wrought iron fence that enclosed St. Mary's carefully groomed lawn and hedges. Tulips in various colors rustled from the breeze as a house finch in a tree gushed forth its rapid series of notes. She had learned about the house finch's song from Parker. He had known all the birds last summer. She had come to recognize a few of the more familiar ones in Aspen.

"I studied wildlife management in college," Parker was telling her the day of the Forest Service party. It had started to drizzle again and he led her through the woods to his house. "That's how I got to know my birds. Ornithology was a required course."

Following behind him, Rhea admired Parker's tall figure, the long legs that plodded through brush, his short blond hair rumpled now from the rain. He had on his dark green Forest Service jacket with the insignia on the shoulder patch. She was excited at the prospect of going to his house. As far as she knew, none of the other women on the district had been to Parker's house.

"Well, here we are," Parker said as they stepped through a clearing. There stood the small log house surrounded by aspen trees. It was one of a cluster of three abodes the government owned and provided for district employees. Impressed by its rustic charm, Rhea eagerly stepped into the kitchen when Parker opened the back door. For a bachelor's house it certainly was tidy, Rhea noticed. The living room was neat and quaintly furnished. Rhea wondered if Parker hired someone to come in each week to clean. Later she found out he did not.

"I'll start a fire," he said and knelt before the fireplace. He began piling wood inside, then looked at her. "Go find something to put on in the bedroom. Before you catch cold. We can dry your pants before you leave."

Rhea must have looked surprised.

Parker smiled as his blue eyes melted into hers. "There are some pants in the closet. They might be too big, but if you prefer, my robe's hanging in the bathroom."

As she slipped into his bedroom, closing the door behind her, Rhea was again stunned at the neatness of the room. The soft ticking of the alarm clock on the headboard of Parker's double bed contrasted with the patter of rain against the walls and roof. Rhea took off her wet jeans and found a pair of Parker's jeans in his closet. She found that they fit her, but she had to roll up the cuffs. Grabbing her wet jeans, she opened the bedroom door and stepped out. Parker had gone out to gather more wood for his tinder box. He had a washer-dryer unit in the kitchen. She threw in her jeans and set it as he walked in with an arm load of damp wood.

"Good, you're my size," he said.

"They're kind of long," said Rhea. She followed him into the living room.

After Parker got the fire going, they sat on the rug in front of it and talked. Parker made some hot chocolate with Amaretto. The sweet drink warmed Rhea from the inside out and she let Parker hold her as they cuddled together, drinks in hand. Staring into the softly dancing flames, the crackle of sparks and burning wood was the only music Rhea wanted to hear.

A yowl from outside summoned Parker to the door. It had grown dark, Rhea noticed, as he let a large, long-haired, ginger tabby cat into the house. The animal was damp and shook itself slightly before staring across the room at Rhea. Then it darted into the kitchen.

"What a beautiful cat," said Rhea. "What's its name?"

"Lynx."

The animal appeared again and sat in the doorway, licking a paw.

Rhea laughed. "Does he give you much trouble?"

"He likes to stay out at night," said Parker. "Not when it's raining, though." He drew her toward him once again. "Lynx is company for me."

Rhea knew it was a hint of Parker's loneliness. She asked, "Do you like living alone?"

He thought a while before answering, "Sometimes."

"Have you always lived alone?"

"No." Rhea listened as Parker told her about his past. He had been married once—at an early age—to a girl who had tricked him into it, claiming he was the father of her child. "She was pregnant," Parker explained. "I thought I was doing the right thing by marrying her. I was even willing to quit college and go to work." He told Rhea he didn't love the girl, and the marriage didn't last. "She had a miscarriage," he said. "Later she began sleeping around with other men and I divorced her. It's a phase of my life I don't like to recall. I didn't like being used."

Rhea guessed that was the reason Parker ignored the flirtations of the women on the Forest Service staff. He was straight and virtuous. He didn't drink, but he did like to keep a bottle of Amaretto on hand for special occasions. His lips brushed her ear and Rhea perked up at once. Wildfire spread throughout her body as she turned her face to meet Parker's. He stared into her eyes and then kissed her. She sensed a passionate need in his long, drawn-out kisses. Overcome by her feelings, she hoped their lovemaking would lead to the bedroom. But for some reason Parker broke off abruptly.

The hum of the dryer kicked off. It was the signal of departure. "Your jeans are dry," said Parker.

"So they are."

Lynx pranced onto Parker's lap just then, which caused them to laugh.

"Lynx to the rescue," said Rhea.

"His timing is unsurpassed," Parker replied. "After you get dressed, I'll drive you home."

The rain had let up and the air was cool and fresh. On the way home Rhea learned Parker loved classical music. He had bought a season pass to the Music Festival. He promised to accompany her to some concerts in the Tent. And he couldn't wait to hear her play.

Rhea climbed the steps to her apartment and sighed as she came out of her reverie. That first evening with Parker Sherwin had been like a dream. If only she had it to do over again ... how differently things might have ended. If only they had known then how little time was left.

6

"*H*ave a good time," Mona called after Rhea as she went out the door. Clad in hiking boots and a rugged pair of blue jeans, Rhea pulled on her backpack with the rolled-up sleeping bag. Two blocks away she caught the shuttle bus to the music campus. The group was to meet there at eleven-thirty.

"There's Rhea now," called out Jerome as she approached the small group of people near the bridge beside the administration building.

Everyone's attention focused on Rhea as she set her things down. Arthur Lawrence, large and stocky with dark hair, a beard and mustache, had wisps of gray at the temples that made him look distinguished. "We're so happy you could join us, dear," said Elizabeth Lawrence. She was a lofty woman with a large bosom and bleached hair. Her makeup was a shade oranger than her skin. Rhea knew Elizabeth Lawrence from her involvement in the Choral Institute last summer. Professor Lawrence was a guest conductor.

"And you already know Oliver and JoAnn," said Jerome.

Rhea greeted the two friends who sat together on the grass, holding hands.

"And this is our daughter, Betsy," said Elizabeth.

"Betsy's joining us as well," Jerome told Rhea with an eager grin.

The Lawrences' teen-age daughter shot a forced smile Rhea's way. She was a cute girl with short blond hair, a slender figure and a turned-up nose. Rhea guessed her to be no older than sixteen. Rhea had the feeling that the Lawrences had forced her to come along.

"Well ..." said Professor Lawrence. He cleared his throat. "We ought to get over to the Snowmass campground, where we are meeting our guide. We can all go in the Bronco."

They collected all their gear and threw it into the back of the Lawrences' Ford Bronco. The three Lawrences sat up front while the other four squeezed into the back seat. Rhea sat pressed between Jerome and the hard metal door as the Bronco bounced along on the road.

"Enough room for you?" asked Jerome.

"I'm fine," said Rhea, offended that Jerome's deodorant had worn off. She rolled the window down a crack for some fresh air.

"Say, isn't this cool?" Jerome continued. "I mean, isn't it great that Betsy could come along?"

It was obvious to Rhea that Jerome had a crush on the Lawrences' daughter. By the looks of it, Oliver and JoAnn were pretty cozy on their side of the seat. Everyone was going to be paired up but her. *This is going to be an interesting trip*, Rhea thought.

Arthur Lawrence drove the Bronco out of Aspen, past the airport, and turned onto Brush Creek Road. Rhea knew Snowmass Village lay ahead. Although she was familiar with the much newer sister ski town, she had never been there. Summer traffic buzzed on both lanes of the winding uphill road. They passed a few elegant-looking homes on the oak brush slopes and marveled at the open meadows and view of the mountains ahead. Residual snow still frosted the highest peak as a few cotton puff clouds lingered in the blue sky.

The village soon came into sight with its clusters of buildings and condominiums spread across the wide green valley. Horses and beefalo grazed next to the rodeo grounds. On the other side of the road people in a golf cart cruised around the edge of a pond on the golf course, and Rhea saw a jogger out for a run along the road.

They passed the ski area and left the condominiums behind as the Bronco turned onto a beat-up road which Professor Lawrence termed "the shortcut." For miles they bounced and plowed over rocks and potholes. Looking behind them, Rhea saw the Snowmass ski area as an expansive slope with its patterns of aspen trees, lifts and ski runs jutting downward. Trees lined the road on either side of them and Rhea wondered how much more of this shaking up the Bronco could stand.

Finally they turned into the Snowmass campground parking lot and Professor Lawrence halted alongside several other vehicles.

"Well, looks like we're not the only ones here," Elizabeth Lawrence commented.

"I'll remind you, this is a holiday weekend," said Jerome.

"This doesn't look like a campground to me," said Betsy.

"Actually, it isn't anymore," said Rhea. "The Forest Service closed the campground several years ago, but everybody still calls it that."

Rhea noticed several horses tied on the other side of the fence, already saddled and bridled. She hoped to get the mellowest one. They were all swishing their tails and looking around as the humans poured out of the Bronco.

"Where is our guide, I wonder," said Professor Lawrence.

"He's over there." Jerome pointed to a man in a cowboy hat.

Rhea pulled her gear from the back of the Bronco as Professor Lawrence walked over to greet the guide.

Jerome offered to carry Betsy's pack for her.

"You don't have to," the girl told him.

"It's my pleasure." Jerome grinned and hoisted up the heavy pack. Betsy regarded him in astonishment.

"Have you ridden before, Rhea?"

Rhea turned to JoAnn, standing next to her. Somehow Mona's sleeping bag had come unrolled. Rhea stooped to fix it. "No, not me," she confessed. "Have you?"

"I've done a little horseback riding. Isn't this something? Imagine, Professor Lawrence hiring an outfitter! Our camp will be all set up for us by the time we get to Snowmass Lake. And I hear the Nickelson Creek Ranch doesn't come cheap."

Rhea looked up in surprise. "The Nickelson Creek Ranch?" she muttered. "Is that where he hired our guide?" She looked over and almost unrolled the sleeping bag again. Trey Michaels was the man wearing the cowboy hat who was attending the horses and talking to Professor Lawrence. He hadn't noticed Rhea yet.

Her pulse leaped. Trey Michaels was their guide!

"Hurry up, Rhea, we're waiting," Elizabeth Lawrence called as the others headed for the horses. Rhea followed with her gear, and suddenly Trey saw her. He looked about as startled as she had been a moment ago. They stared at one another until Professor Lawrence broke the spell.

"Young man, suppose you introduce yourself," the professor told Trey.

Rhea diverted her eyes.

"Hullo, y'all. You can call me Trey. I'm your guide this weekend. I'm going to do everything to see that ya'll have a safe and pleasant ride up to Snowmass Lake and back." He continued on and Rhea noticed the patronizing drawl that had crept into his voice. She cracked a smile to herself. She guessed he talked that way to most tourists as part of the package deal. It was actually rather musical to listen to, she decided.

The group went around and introduced themselves to the guide, and when it was Rhea's turn she hesitated. It seemed unnecessary. She already knew Trey, but she felt reluctant to let the fact be known in front of the others. Before she could open her mouth to speak, Trey cut in.

"And this here can only be the talented Miss Rhea Sinclair," he drawled. "Why, Miss Sinclair, everyone's heard of you."

Rhea swallowed as horror rose from within.

"This lady can play the piano, I'm tellin' you. Why, I've heard her play and she is tops."

What was he doing? Rhea shuddered in embarrassment as the Lawrences stared in amazement.

"I take it you must be referring to the young lady's recent employment at one of the local establishments?" Elizabeth Lawrence asked him.

"Let it be, Liz," chided Professor Lawrence.

Elizabeth sighed. "Oh, Art, people have to make a living one way or another."

Rhea was surprised the Lawrences knew about her job at The Lucky Find, especially considering the short time she had worked there.

"No, ma'am, I wasn't referrin' to that," drawled Trey. He knew how to play up to these people, Rhea knew. "No sir, Mrs. Lawrence, ma'am. I heard Miss Sinclair play in concert. Someday she's going to be famous, I reckon."

Elizabeth Lawrence chuckled. "Young man, I'd hardly dare to say that. But of course *all* our music students are gifted."

To Rhea's relief, Trey quit the contest and helped them mount their horses. When it came Rhea's turn, she turned on him.

"Why did you do that?" she hissed.

Trey was busy untying the reins and didn't look at her. "I was just trying to make a good impression for you."

"These people are sensitive," Rhea whispered fiercely. "Besides, I don't need anybody to butter up my career."

"I'll agree with that. Where'd you ever learn to play like that, anyway? I never saw fingers fly so fast. What was that you were playing?"

The flush returned to Rhea's face. "Mozart," she murmured.

"And I wasn't lyin' when I said you'll be famous," Trey continued. "I mean, that was one fantastic concert ..."

"Stop it!" He was making a mockery out of her. On an impulse Rhea kicked him in the shin. His startled look made her immediately ashamed and she turned away. She hoped no one else had seen.

After she was settled on her horse, Rhea watched Trey go about his work and thought it was going to be a long three days. Rhea's horse, without any persuasion, followed the other horses. She just held on, one hand clutching the saddle horn. This would be no problem, she figured, as long as her horse was content to follow everyone else. She felt awkward and her incompetence showed.

They started up a dirt trail surrounded by aspen trees. Glancing back, Rhea saw Trey riding directly behind her. He announced to the group how he would bring up the rear and be better able to sight any difficulties anyone might have. The horses had been up and down this trail to Snowmass Lake so many times, it was a habit with them, he explained. Rhea noticed how Jerome had managed to ride alongside of Betsy. Trey approached

Rhea on her left and in the back of her mind everything appeared symmetrical.

"You'll be glad you didn't walk when you see what we have to ride up," Trey commented.

Rhea felt shy. She was no longer mad at him for embarrassing her. She looked at him. Under his cowboy hat she saw the glimmer in his brown eyes and remembered the kiss under the porch light. Then, ashamed of herself, she stared ahead. "I wouldn't mind the hike," she told him. "I could hike seven miles easily."

Trey sighed. "Of that I have no doubt," he said. "But even star runners puff and pant their way up this trail."

Rhea smiled. "I take it you've never done it."

"Why, sure I have."

"Without a horse, I mean."

"On my own two feet," he replied, "and with forty or fifty pounds of climbing gear on my back besides."

Rhea looked at him in surprise. "You're a climber?"

"I have climbed," he said.

"Where?"

Trey relaxed with a playful smile. "Around here? Capitol and Pyramid. I've also done some climbing at Yosemite. I don't do much anymore."

Rhea was impressed. "I see."

"Well, I know what you're thinking." He scratched the back of his neck. "You're finding it hard to believe because you can outrun me."

Rhea blushed. "Mountain climbers are supposed to be in good shape," she said.

"Oh, I used to be, but I busted my knee last winter. It happened the last day of ski season."

"Why did you give up jogging?" she asked.

"Who said I gave it up?"

"Well, I haven't seen you out running lately. I thought ..."

"So ... you were lookin' for me." He grinned.

Rhea felt herself getting flustered. "That isn't what I meant. Just ... since I no longer saw you out running ... I mean ..."

"Little lady, you inspire me. Why don't we get together the

next time you're up for a run? I think this time I may surprise you."

Rhea did not reply. The Lawrences were glancing back at them. Then the professor began asking Trey some questions, so he trotted his horse up front for a while. Before long they came to a gate, where Trey dismounted to open it as they all passed through. Rhea preferred to stay last in line. Although the trail was now narrow enough that they had to ride in single file, she wanted to be near Trey. Oliver and JoAnn had taken the lead with the Lawrences behind them. Jerome rode just ahead of Rhea. Every so often he glanced back at her to see how she was coming along, but Jerome's major concern was Betsy, who didn't seem to mind Jerome's mindless chatter and attention.

They encountered several backpackers on the trail heading to Snowmass Lake. Rhea admired the distant peaks as her horse bobbed along beneath her. Here was all this beauty and a perfect afternoon of sunshine. She thought of Parker and their hike up Buckskin Pass last summer. If only he could be here now. How he had loved the wilderness and the challenge of a hike like this one. Rhea was positive Parker had been to Snowmass Lake several times, but he would never have gone on horseback. He would have found it somehow undignified.

She remembered after the Forest Service party how she had trouble keeping her mind on her duties. She was afraid the prickles of joy she felt every time Parker was near would give her away. He, too, seemed preoccupied and would smile at her every so often. Finally he found a chance to be alone with her.

"I've missed you," Parker confided in a low voice when they were sure no one could overhear. "I laid awake for the longest while last Friday night."

Rhea wanted to confess how it had been the same for her. She was in a state of euphoria over this wonderful man who gave her his attention.

"Say, I have to hike up Buckskin Pass next week," Parker continued. "Will you come along?"

Before she could reply, Marie from the front desk summoned

Parker and he departed with a wink. Rhea continued filing reports, but later that day she smiled as she overheard Janet discussing Parker with one of the female seasonals. "Do you notice something different about Parker?"

"Yes, what's got into him?"

"I don't know, but he certainly was in a good mood."

"He didn't even care when I botched up that trail marker at Difficult. He sure is acting weird."

"Maybe he's coming out of his shell."

"You mean … you wish."

"I wonder if he's found himself a girlfriend. What do you think, Rhea?"

Rhea lifted her head and blinked. "What do I think about what?"

"About Parker."

Rhea smiled. "I don't know," she replied.

The other girls didn't suspect. But it grew harder for her and Parker to keep their secret. And when everyone found out Parker had chosen Rhea to accompany him on the day hike to Buckskin Pass, they were envious.

"Why did he choose you?" asked Janet.

"You lucky stiff," said someone else.

"Do you really want to go?" asked another. "I mean, it's not a simple walk by any means. It's straight uphill for three or four hours. I'll gladly go in your place."

But Rhea wouldn't have missed the opportunity for anything. That was the first hint the others got of her developing relationship with the head wilderness ranger. The rumors began, but Rhea no longer cared.

Horses' hooves cloppity-clopped along the trail. The smell of crisp, clear air filled Rhea's nostrils as she reached out to protect her face from a sweep of leaves. They had been traveling on level ground the last hour and were starting to climb. She began to feel hot and sweaty on her thighs and hoped they would stop for a rest soon. Before long someone suggested it and when they came to a little clearing, Trey loped ahead and helped the others off their mounts. Betsy and her mother wandered off into some trees. Trey came over to hold Rhea's horse as she slid off.

"What's the matter?" asked Trey.

Rhea rubbed a leg and groaned. "I'm not used to riding," she said.

"You're sore already? We're not even halfway there."

Rhea noticed the others had scattered, either stretching their legs or taking pictures. She remained near her horse.

Trey held onto three horses. "How does your fiancé feel about you going off without him?"

The question took Rhea by surprise. She didn't know how to answer him at first. "He's … he's not my fiancé ."

"Oh, that's right, I remember now." Trey smiled. "So how does he feel about this trip? Why didn't he come along?"

Now Rhea felt cornered. How was she going to get out of this one? She stared at her feet and said nothing.

After a moment of silence, Trey said, "I reckon I'm treadin' on ground where I'm not wanted." He led the other horses away. In a small desperate way Rhea wanted to cry out to him to wait, but something inside of her let him go. It was better this way. She kept remembering Parker's words, *"He's just a transient …"*

When they started out again, Trey took the lead. Rhea felt stricken with loneliness as she brought up the rear. The chatter and laughter of the others seemed distant and foreign to her. The horses had to cross the beaver pond before they started over the ridge that would take them to their destination. The air felt much colder at this elevation and Rhea noticed her fingers getting puffy. Trey and the pack horses stayed in the water halfway across as— one by one—the others splashed through the pond.

"Trey, what are those mountains over there?" Professor Lawrence indicated snow-covered peaks that rose alongside the ridge.

"Those are part of the West Elk Range," Trey said. "And before long you'll be able to see Snowmass Mountain and Snowmass Lake."

"Fantastic country," remarked Elizabeth Lawrence. "Are we almost there?"

As Rhea's horse passed next to Trey, she glanced at him a moment and as their eyes met she thought she detected a look of knowing. He waited till they were out of the water and then suggested a rest stop.

"But I want to *get* there," complained Betsy. "How much longer is it, anyway?"

"Our horses have some steep climbing ahead," explained Trey. "This is a good place to let 'em rest and drink."

Rhea was relieved to stand on the ground after an especially long ride. She took a long drink of water from her cantine, then stood at the pond's edge, staring into the rocks and tall grasses that poked through the surface.

"Rhea dear, you've been awfully quiet," remarked Elizabeth Lawrence. "Are you feeling all right?"

"I'm fine," Rhea told the older woman. "I'm just a little tired."

"We all are. We didn't realize how far it is. Goodness, I hope we make it there before dark."

"Don't you worry about that, Mrs. Lawrence, ma'am," drawled Trey. "We'll make it in plenty of time. My buddy John's up there right now, fixin' a nice steak dinner for y'all."

Mrs. Lawrence joined her husband as Trey sidled over to Rhea. For a minute the two of them just stood looking out over the water. Rhea was aware of Elizabeth Lawrence's watchful eye and didn't want to give the impression of being overly chummy with the guide.

"Still sore?" Trey asked.

Rhea nodded. If he said anything more about the man in her life, she was sure she would explode.

During the last hitch of their journey up the steep wooded ridge, Rhea rode in the middle of the line and Trey followed everyone with the pack horses bringing up the rear. She felt more at ease now that the conversation drifted all around her. Everyone was growing hungry and joked about how they could smell those T-bones just around the corner.

Rhea glanced behind her several times and caught Trey's encouraging smile. How in control he appeared in his saddle, strong and adept. She could tell he loved the outdoors and the job he was doing, even if it meant putting up with people like the Lawrences now and then.

When they reached the horse camp just below the lake, two horses were hobbled there already as they all dismounted and groaned in relief.

"You folks go ahead and look at the lake," Trey told them. "It's just up the trail." He had to stay and take care of the stock.

Rhea followed Jerome and the others, welcoming the chance to walk. Hikers and campers populated the lake shore. Fancy backpacking tents lay scattered in various colors and people were walking along the shore of the expansive blue-green alpine lake. Rhea was surprised at the large size of the lake with the surrounding mountains that were steep and rocky.

"You can bet that water's too cold to swim in," commented Jerome. Some fishermen were casting their lines a ways off. They walked down to the water's edge and admired the view. The air felt cool and breezy. After several minutes, Rhea followed her group back toward the horse camp to meet Trey and the other guide from Nickelson Creek Ranch. On their way they passed a waterfall that emptied into Snowmass Creek, the stream that ran parallel to the trail.

John Dowd made their acquaintance at the campsite. Three tents had been pitched around a campfire where John had just thrown on the steaks for dinner. The wonderful blend of camp smoke and good beef aroused Rhea's appetite as they approached.

"Why can't we camp closer to the lake?" Elizabeth wanted to know. "Here you can't even see the lake."

John explained that the Forest Service had a regulation about building campfires and that this spot had been designated for that purpose.

"Besides, Liz, it's going to be colder on the lake," Professor Lawrence reminded his wife.

"And more crowded," added John.

Trey had already unloaded their gear near the tents and had left to take the pack horses back to the horse camp.

"Where do we sleep?" JoAnn wanted to know. She yawned. "I may take a short nap before we eat."

The Lawrences had arranged everything in advance. The professor, Elizabeth and Betsy would occupy the largest tent. Oliver and Jerome shared one, and JoAnn and Rhea would sleep in the other. The outfitters had their own tent set up next to the lake. Rhea wasn't sure she felt relieved or disappointed that Trey would not be in the same campsite.

Rhea found the food to be excellent. Tender steaks, complemented by piping hot baked potatoes wrapped in aluminum foil, accompanied cole slaw and French bread. For dessert there was cherry cobbler, baked in a Dutch oven. The outfitters had provided a couple of bottles of a fine French burgundy. Rhea sat between Jerome and JoAnn on the ground as she ate. Trey had found a fallen tree behind her and she felt comfort in his nearness. If Elizabeth Lawrence hadn't been staring at her so much, Rhea might have joined the guide on his perch. She had the feeling that the voice instructor was watching for a reaction so that—Rhea thought—she could later tell her husband, "It's disgusting and loathesome, don't you agree?"

After the meal and the warmth of the wine, it was only natural that a group of music students and faculty would sing around the campfire as it grew dark. Elizabeth started it out and got booed by the rest of them when she wanted to sing opera.

"Everyone knows what a beautiful voice you have," grumbled Arthur, "but not here, Liz. That's not the kind of singing we want to do."

Oliver then began leading with his resonant tenor voice in a round of *Shenandoah*. Rhea sang with the others and didn't notice Trey's absence until he appeared a few minutes later with a guitar. Everyone cheered as he perched himself next to the fire and played and sang. Rhea smiled at him warmly as his eyes met hers.

When the campfire died down and John had packed away the dinner leftovers, the group broke up. It was cold and black and everyone decided to call it a day and retreat to the warmth of their sleeping bags. Rhea listened to the murmur of voices as she crawled into her tent. JoAnn had obviously gone to say goodnight to Oliver. She decided to relieve herself before undressing and found the flashlight. She met JoAnn as she unzipped the tent flap on her way out.

"I'll be right back, JoAnn."

"Don't get lost."

"Don't worry." Rhea's flashlight played over the ground as she wandered a ways. On her way back, she heard footsteps. Lifting her flashlight, she saw a man's form halted just ahead of her.

"Rhea, is that you?" It was Trey.

She flicked off the light and joined him. "Yes. How did you know it was me?"

"I saw you leave camp. Wanna go for a walk?"

Before she could reply, he took her hand firmly in his and pulled her toward the lake. Rhea felt chilled and his closeness soothed her. She let her head rest against his shoulder and he drew his arm around her.

"I didn't know you could sing like that," she told him gently.

"Once in a while I get to showin' off," he replied.

Rhea sighed. "What a beautiful night. Look at those stars."

The lake came into sight and Trey stopped and drew her close. She felt just a trifle afraid of him but didn't want to move away. "Something was bothering you earlier," he said. "What was it?"

Rhea said nothing.

"That other man in your life," he began. "You had a fight with him, didn't you?"

"Trey, please, I don't want to talk about him now."

"I was right. That's why you're depressed."

They walked some more and he held her close. They came to a small dirt cliff overlooking the lake and sat down.

"What's wrong? Did he object to you going on this trip?"

Rhea stared out at the water reflecting the starlight. The moon wasn't out yet and she was glad because she didn't want Trey to see the tears in her eyes. Images of Parker flooded her mind and she felt choked with emotion.

Suddenly Trey kissed her. Blindly and passionately, his lips found hers and her response was equally as passionate. She clung to him and hovered in the glory of his kiss, hesitant to withdraw. Then sobs began to erupt and she pulled away from him.

"What's this?" Trey's finger wiped the wetness from her cheek. "Tears?"

Rhea sniffed, embarrassed to be crying in front of him.

"This guy hurt you. I can see that."

"It's not Parker's fault." Rhea wiped her nose with her sleeve, then pulled away. "I've got to get back. They'll miss me."

"I really don't want you to go," Trey said and kissed her again. It was so comfortable and warm there in his arms. She didn't even mind the horse smell.

"You're making it hard for me, but I *must* go—*now*."

Trey sighed in frustration and rose to his feet, then pulled her up with him. "Okay, but I can't figure you out. How can this guy mean so much to you, yet you can kiss me like that?"

"Parker's ... *dead*." It came out suddenly. Rhea still shuddered to say it out loud, as if by doing so it would be made final. And there was nothing final about her love for Parker. She knew his spirit was very much alive and that he was probably observing everything going on right now.

"What?" Trey either hadn't heard or he disbelieved her.

Rhea couldn't bear to repeat the awful words. She let go of him and began walking back to her tent.

"Rhea, wait!" Trey caught up with her and walked alongside, strangely quiet for several moments. As the glow of the dying campfire came into view, he grabbed hold of her and they stopped. "Why didn't you tell me before? Gosh dang, how was I supposed to know?"

"Well, you know now." Rhea turned away. He hadn't even said how sorry he was. Such disrespect.

"Rhea, is that you?" a woman's voice called from a distance. Elizabeth Lawrence stood outside the tents. Oliver, Jerome and JoAnn were with her.

"Go on," said Trey. The next moment he vanished into the trees.

Rhea hurried over to the group.

"Oh, thank goodness," chided Elizabeth. "We thought something had happened to you."

"I didn't know what to do," apologized JoAnn. "You said you

were coming right back."

"I just went for a walk," said Rhea. Feelings of guilt surfaced.

"Alone?" Elizabeth's voice was accusing.

Before Rhea could respond, Jerome cleared his throat. "Well, let's all hit the sack. I'm up for a hike around the lake tomorrow."

"Oooh, that sounds like fun," said JoAnn.

"I'm sorry I caused you to worry," said Rhea. "It won't happen again." And with that she ducked into her tent. She hadn't fooled Elizabeth Lawrence. The woman undoubtedly knew she had been out with the guide, and by the tone of her voice Rhea decided she would have to be more discreet from now on.

7

*T*he next morning Rhea awoke to the snap of firewood and the smell of smoke and fresh coffee. Cold air on her bare shoulders prompted her to bury into the warmth of her sleeping bag. A mass of tangled dark hair from the other down bag revealed JoAnn, still sound asleep.

Rhea stared up at the ceiling of the tent, where splotches of shadow from the trees left leafy patterns on the orange canvas. Trey had floated in and out of her dreams. She clutched the folds of down as if she were embracing him. She recalled their parting words last night and wondered how he felt about her now that she had told him about Parker.

"Coffee!" someone said outside. "It smells wonderful, John." JoAnn stirred at the sound of Elizabeth Lawrence's resonant voice, which was enough to wake the whole campground.

Rhea unzipped her sleeping bag and shivered as she pulled on her clothes. The cold mountain air had caused droplets of condensation to form on the inside of the tent. She took care not to bump the canvas. Stepping outside, Rhea saw the Lawrences warming themselves next to the fire as John Dowd poured a mug of coffee and handed it to Elizabeth.

"Good morning, Rhea," Professor Lawrence said. "How did you sleep?"

"Very well, thank you."

"Will you have some coffee?" his wife offered.

Rhea crossed her legs. She didn't see Trey up yet. "After I come back." Before they could ask where she was going, she went into the woods to find some camouflage where she could empty her bladder.

When she returned, everybody was up and John busied himself fixing scrambled eggs and bacon over the fire. Trey finally appeared from the horse camp while they ate. Rhea watched as he got a plate from John and dished up the left-overs.

Betsy Lawrence hadn't felt like eating this morning, so Jerome sat beside Rhea. He had been discussing Grieg and the nature theme when Trey came over and sat on the ground between Rhea and Jerome.

"Still planning to hike around the lake?" Trey asked Jerome.

The French horn player wiped egg off his mouth. "Yes, I'm up for it. What about you, Rhea?"

Rhea caught the glint in Trey's eyes. "Okay." Actually, she was eager to exercise her legs.

"Then let's get started as soon as everyone is finished," said Trey. "It's sunny now, but you can never tell when those thunder-heads are goin' to come around."

After breakfast the group started out. Everyone decided to go except John, who preferred to keep an eye on the camp and wash the dishes. He promised to have an appetizing lunch ready when they returned.

"My, but it's brisk this morning," remarked Elizabeth.

"That's not unusual for this time of year, ma'am," said Trey. "Remember, we're at 11,000 feet." He and Rhea followed the rest. JoAnn and Oliver led the way and Betsy was being pursued by the undaunted Jerome.

"Looks like the lake is still partially frozen," said Professor Lawrence.

Rhea noticed the Lawrences' daughter had dressed in only shorts and a windbreaker over her T-shirt. "Won't Betsy get cold?" she asked.

"I'm sure it will warm up," said Elizabeth. "After all, it is July."

"I tried to tell her to wear something warmer," grumbled Professor Lawrence, "but she never listens."

Elizabeth Lawrence leaned close to Rhea and whispered in her ear. "Betsy woke up with her period. She's not in a very good mood."

Rhea didn't comment. The sun *might* warm things up. She had bundled up in a warm coat. Parker's influence had taught her never to take these mountains for granted at any time of the year. She knew Betsy would be sorry later.

When the Lawrences were well ahead of them, Rhea turned to Trey behind her. "I didn't mean to be a crybaby last night."

He came up beside her. "Don't give it a second thought." He took her hand and squeezed it. His hand felt warm and strong in hers and she didn't care who saw them.

Rhea looked at the crystal blue sky. It was a gorgeous day. Up ahead Elizabeth Lawrence turned around to stare at the two of them, hand in hand. But Rhea no longer cared what the woman thought.

After a while the climbing started getting rugged and Rhea let go of Trey's hand, but he stayed close to her. They rested often because the others in the group—particularly Jerome and the older couple—found the walk strenuous. Rhea stared out toward Buckskin Mountain during one of their rest stops. She remembered she had stood there a year ago and Parker had pointed out Snowmass Lake to her. Someday they had planned to hike to where she was sitting right now.

The hike up Buckskin Pass with Parker had turned out to be more than Rhea had bargained for. Where Parker was used to strenuous backcountry terrain, Rhea had to push herself constantly to keep up. By the time they reached the top, Rhea was exhausted. Parker patiently let her rest in a grassy field after they ate their packed lunch. She fell asleep in the beating rays of the sun and awoke with Parker seated next to her. The wind blew his blond hair. He didn't appear tired at all.

"Are you sorry you came with me?" he asked.

"No. I'll survive."

"It'll be easier going down."

"I know."

He caressed her cheek. "I'm afraid you've had more than your share of sun."

The view of the mountainscape captivated Rhea. They could

see for miles. Parker took her into his arms then and it was heaven to rest against him as the wind tousled their hair.

"All week you've been on my mind," he told her. "Nothing's been normal. I lie awake in bed. I haven't had much appetite. I couldn't wait for this day when we could finally be alone together again."

"I know," replied Rhea. "The girls in the office have been concerned about you."

Parker smiled. "Maybe it's time we really gave the hens something to cackle about." He kissed her, then said, "Let's start down now. When we get to Aspen, we'll go somewhere for a bite to eat."

But after they reached the Maroon Bells parking lot later that afternoon, Rhea's blisters hurt so much and she was so tired, they decided to postpone their plans. Parker drove her home, where she went to bed at seven, sore but happy.

"Rhea, are you coming? Or are you going to sit there day-dreaming?"

Rhea glanced up, startled out of her memories. Trey reached for her hand and they followed the others. Betsy griped to her mother and Elizabeth tried to console the girl. *What a drag to get up into the wilderness and have it be that time of the month*, Rhea thought.

Jerome puffed and wheezed when they stopped to rest again. He seemed to be short of breath and was more pooped than anyone else. Rhea was concerned about him and left Trey's side to talk to him.

"I'm hanging on," Jerome told her in a strained voice. "Don't worry about me, Rhea."

Nevertheless, Rhea worried. Jerome did not usually complain, but he *was* overweight.

"Mother, don't bug me!" Betsy shouted.

Elizabeth was having another spat with the teenager. "I don't like your tone, young lady."

"Why don't you just tell the whole world?" Betsy fired. "You may as well. Everyone here knows I've got my period!"

"Keep your voice down!"

"Keep *my* voice down?" Betsy laughed. "That's an impossible feat! I am your daughter, after all!"

"Betsy, that's enough," scolded Professor Lawrence.

"I didn't even want to come on this trip!"

"I said that's enough. Let's not spoil it for the others."

"Well, then I won't!" Betsy stalked toward the woods.

"Where are you going?" called Elizabeth. But Betsy didn't answer. She ran out of sight.

"Betsy, come back!" shouted the professor.

Elizabeth turned away. "Oh, let her go, Art."

Professor Lawrence frowned at his wife. "We can't let her take off into the woods like that."

"She's just throwing one of her tantrums. She'll rejoin us when she cools down."

"For heaven's sake, she's no longer a two-year-old," grumbled the professor.

Jerome got to his feet then. "I'll go after her," he volunteered. He started off toward the woods.

"Jerome, wait!" cried Rhea. "Maybe you shouldn't."

"Somebody's got to watch after her," he replied. "She can't be far." He disappeared into the trees as Trey and the others joined them. Rhea explained what happened with Betsy.

"Why didn't you stop her?" demanded Trey. "Where did she go?"

"We tried to stop her," said the professor. "I'm afraid our daughter is too headstrong for her own good."

"Gol' dang, it's stupid leavin' the trail," Trey cried. "You all better wait right here. I'd better go after her."

Rhea told him that Jerome had already gone after Betsy. "They can't get lost," she added.

Trey looked around. He was obviously not happy about the situation, but finally relaxed. "Well, all right, but I hope they don't do anything stupid."

"If I know Betsy, she'll be back at the campsite long before we are," said Elizabeth.

A couple of hours later, when they reached the campground and were tired and hungry, they found the 16-year-old sitting with

John. Betsy grinned at them. "How was your walk?" she asked.

"Well, thank goodness you're back." Elizabeth was too worn out to scold the girl.

"I returned half an hour ago," Betsy boasted. "I've been helping John with lunch." She put her arms around the outfitter. *What a brat*, Rhea thought.

"Where's Jerome?" Rhea looked around. She expected her heavy friend to emerge from his tent.

"Not here," replied John. "Wasn't he with you?"

"You mean, he's not back?" Rhea grew alarmed.

"Why, no."

"Betsy, didn't you see Jerome?" asked Professor Lawrence.

The girl tossed her head. "Should I have?"

"The poor boy went to find you," said Elizabeth. "You shouldn't have taken off in the first place."

Betsy hung her head.

"Well, I'm sure he'll be along shortly," said Elizabeth. "Let's eat that wonderful lunch you promised us, John."

While everyone else went about getting ready to eat, Rhea stood where she was, a trifle concerned. When Trey returned from checking the horses, she told him she was worried about Jerome.

"Grab a bite to eat. I'll go get a horse," said Trey.

But Rhea wasn't hungry. Everyone looked up from eating when Trey came into camp, leading the horse.

"What are you doin', Trey?" asked John.

"The little lady's worried about her friend." Trey winked at Rhea. "We're goin' to have a look-see." He gave the horse to Rhea to hold while he gathered a blanket and first aid kit. Then they started back toward the lake.

Even with the horse that Trey led behind him, they were able to move quickly toward the spot where they had last seen Jerome disappear into the trees. Rhea noticed the sky had collected a blanket of clouds in the last hour. When the sun was hidden, the wind off Snowmass Lake blew like ice against her exposed skin. But as long as they kept moving, she didn't feel cold.

"Isn't this where it was?" asked Rhea.

"I think you're right." Trey tied the horse to a tree stump.

"Let's hope your friend knew enough to head back toward camp. With rain headin' this way, I'd hate to think of him wanderin' off toward Lost Remuda Lake."

Rhea started toward the trees. "I remember Parker said somebody died up there last summer."

"That's nothin' new," said Trey. "People get into trouble in the mountains all the time."

Rhea began shouting Jerome's name. Trey told her to comb just the immediate area and he'd return in five minutes. She continued to call for Jerome. They continued in this fashion for another half hour or so. It started to drizzle.

Rhea zippered her coat up all the way and shivered, waiting for Trey to return again. It was quite possible the French horn player had reached camp by now. She pulled on her wool mittens and started walking again when she suddenly heard a human sound nearby.

"Jerome?" Rhea cried out.

Somebody moaned. Rhea followed the direction of the sound down a grassy embankment and discovered her friend writhing in the bushes.

"Jerome!" She scrambled down to him and saw that he was conscious but slightly incoherent. There was a glassy look in his pale blue eyes and his glasses had fallen off. She saw them a few yards away and went to retrieve them. "Jerome, what happened? Are you hurt?"

The man tried to speak but his voice wavered. "Practice ... I'm late."

Rhea noticed a blue tinge of color in Jerome's lips. He was shaking. "Jerome, did you fall? Can you walk?"

He tried to get up. "I've got practice," he said. "Help me up." Then he howled in pain and fell back, grabbing his foot.

Oh no, thought Rhea, *he's fallen and broken his leg.* Worse than that, he was suffering from hypothermia. No telling how long he had been lying there and he hadn't thought to bring anything to keep warm. He was disoriented and confused—telltale signs that his body temperature was falling rapidly. It was probably a good thing he couldn't move with that foot or he might have wandered off to who-knows-where.

"Jerome, I'll be right back. I'm going to find Trey."

"Rhea ... can you help me?" Jerome pleaded. "Rhea, don't go yet. Wait for me." Again he tried to move and collapsed in agony.

Rhea removed her coat and threw it over Jerome's shoulders. Then she stumbled up the embankment and yelled for Trey. To her relief, he came right away. Without having to explain, Rhea turned and ran back down the embankment.

"There you are," cried Jerome as they approached him. "You forgot your jacket, Rhea."

Trey knelt beside Jerome and felt the foot. Jerome groaned and shivered.

"Is it broken?" Rhea asked. She hugged herself for warmth.

"Don't think so," said Trey. "Probably a sprain. Can you go bring the horse?"

Rhea left immediately. She ran as a cold rain fell. Her thoughts were focused on Jerome. Thank goodness Trey had brought the horse. It would be difficult to carry someone of Jerome's immense size back to camp without it.

By the time she returned with the horse, Trey had bundled Jerome in both their coats. He reached for the blanket and first aid kit. Rhea watched as Trey wrapped the ankle. Jerome sat with all the covers around him, his eyes closed. It scared Rhea to see him that way. Would he be all right? Perhaps they'd have to take him down from the lake. What a way to end their trip.

Trey finished bandaging the ankle and Jerome opened his eyes and recognized Rhea. "Hello," he said.

"Jerome, how do you feel?"

"Kind of strange."

"Okay, big fella. Let's get you onto the horse." Trey helped Jerome to his feet. Rhea also helped to steady him. It was a chore, but at least Jerome cooperated with them. He no longer seemed to be confused.

Rhea welcomed her coat back as they headed for camp. She and Trey walked along on either side of the horse just in case Jerome started to fall off the saddle. The rain let up by the time they approached the campground.

Jerome became the center of attention and John Dowd checked him over as everyone gathered around. They decided it would be best to take Jerome down, but the heavy young man had recovered his dignity over a hot cup of coffee. Resembling a hooded monk in the blanket, he smiled at them. "I'll be fine. I feel much better, thanks to Trey and Rhea. I don't want to go down."

"Hey, bud, it's for your own good," John advised.

"You could use a warm bed tonight," added Trey.

"Really, I'll be all right."

After much protesting, John finally gave in. "Well, maybe it's all right he stays the night. Luckily you got to him before he was too bad off."

"I don't see why everyone is making such a fuss," said Jerome.

Rhea smiled at him. It was obvious he enjoyed all of this attention. She spent the rest of the afternoon at Jerome's side, filling him with hot drinks and food. She didn't see much of Trey. The others were tired out from the walk. The Lawrences took a nap and Betsy hung around John. She had said barely a word to Jerome. Rhea guessed the girl was probably embarrassed since she had been the cause of Jerome going off and spraining his ankle. She noticed Oliver and JoAnn were spending a lot of time alone, smooching a lot when they thought no one was looking.

Around the campfire that evening, John and Trey took turns telling stories. Betsy had given up on John and was now flirting with Trey. Rhea couldn't help feeling annoyed and uncomfortable as she watched Betsy try to sit as close as she could to Trey. Anxiety began to seep in as she watched the flicker of firelight play on Trey's face. He didn't seem to mind the young girl's flirtations. A sinking feeling hit her each time she heard their mingled laughter and as the evening progressed Trey appeared to notice Rhea less and less.

When it was again John's turn to tell a story, Trey excused himself and left. Rhea was quick to notice Betsy sneak away a minute later. She pretended to act as if nothing was wrong, but all she could think about was last night and the time she had spent alone with Trey. She felt sick at heart because this was their last night at Snowmass Lake and somehow she had wanted it to be special. She certainly hadn't expected Trey to trot off in the dark with Betsy Lawrence.

Yet somehow Rhea realized this must be what Trey was really like. He was probably used to a different girl every night. Trey Michaels was not like Parker. No man was like Parker.

After the hike to Buckskin Pass, Rhea's and Parker's courtship had been in full swing. She remembered the night he had taken her out to dinner and he had seen her in a dress for the first time. They sat in one of Aspen's finer restaurants. The private table and candlelight enhanced the splendor Rhea felt in being there with this man who was fast becoming the focus of her life.

Parker reached for her wrist across the table and smiled as she sipped wine. "You look lovely tonight."

Rhea smiled at him and lifted her wine glass, relaxed by the warm, gentle strokes of his fingers against hers. She felt the waves of desire when he gazed into her eyes and she knew in her heart she would give anything to this man. She would give her entire life to him, she decided.

Parker wanted to hear her play the piano, so Rhea brought him to the apartment afterwards. She apologized for the piano being in her bedroom, but he understood. Since there was nowhere else to sit, he stretched out on her bed and asked her to begin playing.

"What would you like to hear?" she asked him.

"You choose something."

Rhea impressed him with some Debussy. She could hardly believe it when Parker told her afterwards that he, too, had always loved the music of the radical French composer. For an encore she unmasked all of her inhibitions in the tender and emotional *"La Fille aux cheveux de lin"* from the First Book of Preludes.

Parker gazed at her as she finished. "That was wonderful," he said. He stood up and ran his hand through her hair and she turned to smile at him. When he kissed her, she sensed an over-whelming need in him. Their embraces grew more passionate until they collapsed upon Rhea's bed. But then, suddenly Parker pulled away.

"We don't have to worry about Mona," Rhea told Parker. "She works late. Sometimes she doesn't come home at all." But after a tense silence Rhea realized nothing was going to happen. The last thing she wanted to do was press him into lovemaking when he had spent so many years avoiding promiscuous women and not knowing whom he could trust.

Parker sighed and said, "The weekend's ahead of us. How would you like to start running with me?"

Rhea made a joke out of it. "Why? Are you campaigning for the fall election?"

"Seriously, Rhea."

"Well, okay," she said reluctantly. "But it's not late. Stay longer."

He got up from the bed and pulled her to her feet. Then he took her into his arms once again. "I love you, Rhea."

"I love you, Parker," she whispered. She asked him again to stay, but he didn't. She knew better than to press her luck. He needed time. She had been positive that soon things would be different. And, of course, they never were.

John's story ended and Rhea returned to the present. Everyone was getting up to turn in for the night. Her heart felt laden with sadness. Elizabeth Lawrence complained of stiff legs and the professor called for Betsy.

"I think she headed for the horse camp," said Jerome. "Trey went to check on the horses."

Rhea turned away.

"You sure you're going to be warm enough tonight?" John asked Jerome.

The French horn player insisted he was fine, then put a restraining hand on Rhea's shoulder as she passed. "Rhea, everything okay?"

"Yes, Jerome." Rhea sniffed. "Some smoke got in my eyes. Good night." Then she darted toward her tent before anyone else could question her.

JoAnn wasn't in their tent. Rhea figured her tentmate was out on a moonlight walk with Oliver, just as Trey and Betsy must be. The idea churned within her and she cast off her clothes and burrowed into the sleeping bag. The tears came then and she smothered her sobs in the pillow.

She was doomed to be a loner, just like Jerome—only he didn't seem too disturbed at being ignored by Betsy. *The little stuck-up bitch*, Rhea thought. How could Trey be so blind?

Rhea froze as the tent flap unzipped. She lay face down and quickly pulled the covers up over her head. JoAnn would think she was asleep. No one would know she had been crying. Rhea took deep breaths and waited. JoAnn was certainly taking her time getting ready for bed—or was she just sitting there? Rhea didn't hear the familiar rustle of clothing or the crackle of JoAnn's hairbrush. At least the other woman was courteous enough not to speak.

Suddenly something touched Rhea's hair. Startled, she remained still, but became alarmed when a hand fondled a long lock of her hair. *What does JoAnn think she's doing?* Rhea rolled over and opened her eyes. There was a man in her tent at her side.

"Oh!" Rhea gasped.

"Shh!" It was Trey.

Rhea sat up, relieved that it was him, but not understanding why he was there. "Trey, what are you doing?" Aware of her naked state, she pulled the sleeping bag up to her neck.

"Quiet," he whispered. "It's a conspiracy."

"What is?"

Trey leaned closer. She could smell the hay and his nearness excited her. "JoAnn and Oliver," he whispered. "John and I are letting them use our tent."

"What?" Then Rhea burst out giggling.

"John's in Jerome's tent," explained Trey. "I had nowhere to go. Do you mind?"

Rhea relaxed. She was glad for his company. "What about Betsy?" she asked.

"What about her?" Trey replied. "She's in her parents' tent like she should be."

"No, I meant … you and her."

Trey hesitated. "I don't catch your drift." Then he asked, "Hey, are you jealous?"

Rhea turned away, humiliated. "Why don't you go join John and Jerome?"

"Are you kidding? It's crowded in that tent with just your friend."

The way Trey said *your friend* struck a chord in Rhea. She looked at him. "Wait a minute. Are *you* jealous?" she asked.

"Me? Why?"

"Trey, don't be ridiculous. Jerome is one of my closest, dearest friends, but he could never be … what you're thinking."

Trey sighed. "Well, didn't he ask you to come on this trip? I figured …"

"You figured wrong," she said. "Jerome is … he's like my brother. There's never been anything between us. Honest."

"Well, the same holds true for Betsy," said Trey. "She's a child … and a rather spoiled one at that." After a pause he said, "JoAnn and Oliver could be a while. Mind if I stay till she returns?"

"What will Mr. and Mrs. Lawrence say?"

"Who cares? Let me in."

"What?"

"It's cold out here."

Rhea unzipped her sleeping bag and moved aside. "I'm not sure there's room for both of us."

"There's room enough." Trey removed his boots and poked his legs down into the warmth. With his hand he explored the smooth contour of her naked hips and waist. Gently he touched each breast and moved closer to share the warmth.

Then Trey kissed her. Rhea's heart pounded. As much as she wanted the closeness, she wasn't sure about anything else. She tensed up.

"What's the matter?" he asked. "You been cryin' again?"

Rhea sniffed. "I'm okay now."

"How long do you plan to stay in mourning?" he asked.

"I … I don't know what you mean."

"Over this guy. How long do you intend to go on making your-self miserable?"

"I'm not miserable."

"You are so."

She sniffed again and tried to think of something to steer the conversation away from Parker. Trey had no right to be so unfeeling.

"I mean," Trey continued, "it's one thing to be in competition with somebody, but I don't like playing second fiddle to a dead guy."

Rhea felt she had to change the subject. "Why did you leave the concert?" she asked.

"Huh? What concert?" Then Trey remembered. "Oh, that."

"I waited for you afterwards, but you left."

"I would've stayed, but I was on my lunch hour. And if I didn't mention it earlier, I got a kick out of hearing you play that Snydley Whiplash music."

Rhea laughed. "That was Mozart."

Trey pulled the sleeping bag over both their heads, then held her very close and she let him kiss her again. Snuggled against him, Rhea felt warm, safe and happy. She was aware of her bare skin and growing sensations of uncontrollable desire.

"I want to make love to you," Trey whispered.

Rhea couldn't believe he was asking. "You ... do?"

"You know I do, and you want it too." He began fondling her and kissing her neck and shoulder, which sent tingles of pleasure throughout her body. Rhea wanted to give in. Every fiber of her being felt ready. How easy it would be just to let it happen, here and now. But she remembered where she was and the people she had come with.

"It's too risky. Someone might hear," she said. "Suppose JoAnn comes back and finds us?"

Trey relinquished and lay back with his arm wrapped around her. "Okay, you win." He sighed.

They remained in each others' arms, but said little. Rhea didn't want to think about JoAnn's return. She wished Trey could stay till morning. After a while sleep overcame her.

When Rhea awoke, it was dawn and JoAnn had entered the tent. Trey was already awake and sat up. He climbed out of the sleeping bag and put on his boots.

JoAnn whispered her apologies as Trey finished getting dressed. Rhea sat up and smoothed her hair. She was weary and wanted to go back to sleep, but she moved toward Trey with the sleeping bag wrapped around her. She didn't care what JoAnn thought. As Trey stepped outside the tent, Rhea poked her head out and Trey bent down and kissed her once more.

"Good night," he whispered.

Rhea told him good night, although it seemed a little odd with the first light of day coming through the trees in the direction of the lake. As he stumbled away, she was startled to notice a head suddenly draw back inside the Lawrences' tent. She thought it was the professor. Apparently he had awakened and seen Trey leave the girls' tent.

Rhea zipped the tent flap shut again, too groggy to worry about getting expelled from the music school.

8

*A*s they rode down from Snowmass Lake later that morning, Rhea remained quiet and serene. She felt content just to ride, take in the scenery and the fresh forest smells. She definitely felt stiffness in her thighs from her horse. Trey led the way and Rhea admired his well-developed shoulders and slender build. She remembered how good it had felt lying beside him in the sleeping bag.

By noon they reached the trailhead. Like everyone else, Rhea looked forward to going home and taking a shower. Trey helped John unload packs, then came over to say goodbye to her.

"I'll call you when I get a chance," he said.

Rhea smiled. "Okay," then she added, "I enjoyed myself."

"Good. We'll do it again sometime." Then he lowered his voice and leaned toward her. "Only next time with not so many folks around."

When Rhea arrived home, Mona was still in bed. Rhea set her things down and headed for the shower. When she came out, she found her roommate in the kitchen drinking a cup of coffee.

"How was it?" asked Mona.

"Fantastic." Rhea unwrapped the towel from her head and shook her wet, tangled hair.

"Oh-oh." Mona stared at her. "Something happened."

"What do you mean?"

"You have the symptoms."

"Mona, I don't know what you're talking about."

"Something must have happened to you at Snowmass Lake," said Mona. "I can see it in your face."

"What are you talking about?" asked Rhea.

"I've seen it before," said Mona. "Last summer with Parker—starry eyes ... floating on Cloud Nine ... humming in the shower. Rhea Sinclair, you're in love!"

Rhea sat down at the table. "And who am I supposed to be in love with?"

"That's what you're supposed to tell me!"

Rhea touched her wet hair. "Well, there's no sense in trying to hide it." She smiled. "A certain guide the Lawrences hired from Nickelson Creek Ranch."

"I was right. Trey Michaels!"

"Yes." There. She had admitted it out loud. *Was it possible?* she wondered. Was *she*—Rhea Sinclair—falling in love with Trey Michaels? Remembering the intimacy they had shared last night, suddenly the idea didn't strike her as being absurd.

Later on, as Rhea brushed out her damp tresses in front of her mirror, she thought about Trey. He had promised to call her when he got a chance. She hoped it would be today.

Rhea wheeled her bike onto Bleeker Street after slipping into her jogging clothes. Suddenly Parker's voice permeated her thoughts.

"*How did your weekend go in the wilderness?*" he asked. He ran alongside her bike and Rhea slowed so that Parker's spirit could keep up. It surprised her that he should ask. Certainly he must know everything that had gone on.

"It was okay," she told him in her thoughts.

"*Just ... okay?*"

"Why are you asking?" His presence made her feel uncomfortable all of a sudden.

Parker said nothing until she reached the river and locked her bike up at the bridge. Then he asked, "*Would you rather run by yourself?*"

Rhea stared at him and—to her astonishment—her heart went out to him as she began stretching before her run. "No, Parker, please don't go."

They started to jog, side by side. She sensed worry in him. "I'm sorry if I disappointed you, Parker."

He grinned at her as they bounced along. *"You could never disappoint me, Rhea. Don't you realize I love you?"*

Rhea welcomed his words. The warmth in his blue eyes caused her to smile at him. She knew their love was real. That hadn't changed and it never would.

When she got home after jogging, Rhea fixed herself supper. Mona was out for the evening, but had left a note saying Rhea's parents had phoned. Rhea didn't feel like calling them. She already knew how the conversation would go. They'd start asking about school and her new job. In her last letter home she had told them about the piano bar. Then they'd find out she had lost her job, wasn't working, and that she was in need of money.

Reminded of her depleting financial state, Rhea sat on the balcony when it grew dark. She didn't know what to do about her bills. Mona hadn't bugged her about the rent money yet, even though it was several days late.

Trey didn't call and she felt let down after the eventful weekend. Suddenly here she was, alone, with only her piano for company. And for some reason she didn't feel like playing it. The flute student downstairs began a delightful series of trills and Rhea listened, soothed by the liquid tones. The stars shone brightly against the outline of Ajax Mountain.

Rhea remembered how she had spent many evenings last summer under the stars over at Parker's house. After the night she had played for Parker in her apartment, Rhea spent every free evening with him. She felt at first that she was neglecting her piano, but her music really hadn't suffered. Parker even suggested that being away from the piano may have been a help. She knew that, if given a choice, she would choose Parker over the piano anytime.

One warm evening last summer in late July, Rhea relaxed with Parker in his back yard. They sat side by side, facing the woods and watched the stars as they listened to the crickets. Rhea enjoyed the cool air after another ninety-degree day in a heat wave. In one of the nearby government houses, rock music boomed and they could hear occasional laughter.

"Sounds like the seasonals are having a party tonight," Rhea remarked.

"One of the guys got a keg," said Parker. "Reminds me too much of college days."

Rhea touched Parker's hand and he closed his fingers over hers. "You should hear what they say about us," she told him.

"Who?"

"The Forest Service women. Or haven't you noticed them?"

"Not much," he admitted.

Rhea rested her head against his shoulder. "Oh, Parker, how could you not notice? They're always gossiping." She hesitated, then said, "They think we're sleeping together."

"And how would you feel if we were?" he asked softly.

Rhea wasn't sure what he meant by the question. "It doesn't bother me what anybody thinks. It's not important."

"No, I mean ... how would you feel about us ... I mean, if we were ... sleeping together?"

For a few thrilling moments as she gazed up into his face, Rhea wondered if he was going to break his own rule and take her to bed. She decided to be honest with him. "Life would be perfect," she murmured.

Parker gathered her into his arms then and kissed her. "If only you knew just how much I want that to happen."

"Then ... let it happen."

He then took her two hands in his and smiled. "I love you and it's hard not to when you are so beautiful and loving toward me. But you must preserve your virtue until we are married."

Rhea continued to be perplexed by his attitude. Certainly in this day and age Parker must be mocking her. But she couldn't be sure. She opened her mouth to respond, but caught the sparkle in his blue eyes.

"Rhea," he said, "will you marry me?"

Her look of surprise was brief. A moment later she kissed him. "You know I will." She laughed. She didn't even have to think it over. "When?" she asked.

"Oh, I don't care. How soon would you like to get married?"

"I think a summer wedding would be nice," she said. Besides, if he was going to make her wait until their wedding night to make love, she saw no reason why they should delay their plans.

"That doesn't give us much time," said Parker. "Let's wait till the end of September, when the trees are in full color. It's the most beautiful time of the year here." He also mentioned that his family would probably want to come, and certainly Rhea's parents as well.

So Rhea consented and they set the date that night for September 30. Together they studied the stars, oblivious to the rock and roll next door, secure and happy in each other's arms.

Classes and piano practice took up most the next day. Rhea had been thinking about her financial state, so as soon as she got home she went through the help wanted ads in the *Aspen Times*. Nothing appealed to her. There were plenty of restaurant openings, desk clerk jobs and bank teller positions, but most of them were full time.

She sighed and put the paper down. Hopefully the next paper would be more promising. The piano bar job would have been okay had it worked out. But there was no way she was going to go back to The Lucky Find and put up with Mr. Cox.

The doorbell rang. Rhea suddenly remembered that Jerome might drop by with a piano accompaniment he wanted her to tape for him. When she answered the door, she was startled to find Trey dressed in jogging attire.

"Are you up for a run along the Rio Grande?" he asked.

Rhea scanned his red and black Lycras. The outfit appeared new and fit him well. "Now?"

"Sure, why not?" He hopped from foot to foot.

Rhea laughed and invited him in. She had planned to run at dusk, but because he was ready to go, she decided to put off her homework till later. She quickly went to her bedroom and changed.

When she emerged in her shorts and a T-shirt, she noticed Trey examining a photo in a glass frame—one of many she kept of Parker around the apartment. He set the picture down and his eyes moved over her in approval.

"Let's go," said Rhea. They left without a word about the photo. Once they reached the jogging trail, they stretched and prepared for their run. Rhea tried to decide whether she should go easy on Trey or give him a run for his money. Suddenly she noticed Parker's spirit beside her.

They started out, Trey on Rhea's left and Parker close on her right side. Parker grinned, but said nothing as Rhea stared straight ahead, settling into a fast but comfortable pace.

"How long you been doin' this?" Trey asked.

"About a year," she said.

"Do you ski?" he asked.

So far Trey had kept up with her. Rhea shook her head. "Me? Ski? Never."

"It's not a dirty word, you know. After all, this is Aspen."

Rhea smiled. "I know, and if you live in Aspen you're supposed to ski."

"That's right."

"Well, I don't." Then she turned to him. "I suppose you ski."

"That's the reason I came to Aspen," said Trey. "There ain't that much snow in Texas, and bull shit isn't white."

Rhea noticed Parker's smug look. *"One of those transient ski bums,"* she heard him say. *"Didn't I tell you, Rhea?"*

"Well, I don't ski," Rhea said again, "and I don't intend to learn."

"Aw, Rhea, you don't know what you're missing," said Trey. "This winter I'll teach you." After a pause he said, "Actually, you might like cross-country better. Ever tried that?"

Rhea admitted she hadn't. Trey began telling her about the telemarking sport. Rhea listened, amazed that he could talk so much and keep running at the steady pace she had set. He should have been starting to get winded and fall behind.

"You've improved," she commented when they passed the one-mile marker. "I'm impressed."

Trey's breathing grew labored now but he still did not let up. "I've been working out at the club a lot."

"Where?"

"The Snowmass Club," he said. Then he added, "I live in

Snowmass Village." He then told her he had spent the last week and a half working out hard in order to be a better running partner for her.

Rhea ignored Parker's smirk. She learned that Trey was house-sitting for some rich people who owned a vacation home in Melton Ranch. They turned around at the Slaughterhouse Bridge and Rhea saw that Trey was still going strong. Parker's spirit continued to run silently on her right side. Suddenly he spoke up.

"Hey, why don't we sprint the last half mile?" Parker suggested.

Rhea turned to him. "You mean ... race?" she asked in her head.

"Don't you want to show him up?" asked Parker.

"I don't know." Rhea noticed that Trey was starting to get tired. What a cruel trick it would be to leave him behind after he had proved he could keep up with her this far.

"Go on," urged Parker. *"Ask him."*

"Parker, I don't know about this."

"Why are we slowing down?" Trey asked.

Rhea saw the mile marker ahead. She grinned at Trey. "I'll race you to the end."

"What!"

"Come on!" She charged ahead and Parker was beside her, laughing. They had taken Trey by surprise. Rhea glanced back and saw him sprinting toward her. As the bridge came into sight, Trey burst forward and they crossed the finish line together.

They staggered to a walk, both of them wheezing and panting. Rhea looked over her shoulder and saw Parker far behind. He hadn't been able to keep up.

"Lady, that was one hell of a run!" Trey clutched the bridge railing to catch his breath.

"I just ... had to know ... if you really were ... in shape," said Rhea. She no longer saw any trace of Parker on the jogging trail. He had vanished from sight.

"Did I disappoint you?" Trey pushed his wavy brown hair off his wet forehead.

Rhea only smiled as they headed back up the hill.

9

"*I* have to be gone most the week," Trey said when they reached Rhea's apartment. "We have a long trip booked in the Sopris area. I won't be able to see you till after the weekend."

Rhea unlocked the door to her apartment and they went in.

"So," Trey resumed, "how about we go somewhere tonight?"

Rhea agreed and told him she'd grab a shower and be ready in fifteen minutes. Later, they climbed into Trey's blue pickup truck, which still had the hay and leather smell. Rhea drank it in through her nostrils and realized she actually liked the smell. Trey started the engine.

"I hope you don't mind if we drop by my place first."

"I don't mind at all," said Rhea.

He reached over and touched his lips to hers, which sent shivers up her spine.

On the way to Snowmass Village Rhea mentioned to Trey that she was looking for a part-time job. "There just doesn't seem to be a thing suitable," she said. "I hate the thought of having to give piano lessons again."

"What's wrong with that?"

"Nothing, I suppose. It got me through the winter. I just need a change."

"I reckon The Lucky Find wasn't challenging enough?"

Rhea stared out the window as they swerved around the curve at Shale Bluffs. "It was lousy pay."

"Not to mention the lousy fringe benefits," he added. "Don't feel bad, little darlin', you're not the first one to run into that particular situation."

"Oh, I know that. But where am I going to find work now?"

Trey said he'd talk to John Dowd. "We can always use some-body to shovel out the stables." When Rhea looked shocked, he poked her playfully. "Only kiddin'."

When they turned into the Melton Ranch subdivision some time later, Rhea admired the lovely homes that overlooked Brush Creek Valley. They wound their way up further, then Trey parked before a large tri-level solar home with enormous tinted windows. The garage could hold at least three vehicles and the back lawn sloped upward into an oak brush field with a few clustered aspens.

"Like it?" asked Trey.

"You have this whole place to yourself?" cried Rhea.

"Yup. It's got five bedrooms and four bathrooms." Trey got out and she waited till he came around to open her door. "There's a hot tub too."

Rhea walked with him up to the house, fascinated by its ultra-modern architecture. She couldn't imagine visiting such a house, let alone living in one like Trey did. "Do you pay rent?" she asked.

"Nope. The owners are glad to have me here lookin' after the place for them."

"But what do you do when the owners are here?"

Trey unlocked the garage and they entered through it. "They say they don't mind my stayin' around while they're here, but I usually make myself scarce."

"That's a rather unusual arrangement, isn't it?" asked Rhea. "I mean, I've heard that most people who house-sit get booted out every year around Christmas time."

"Not the case here," said Trey. He told her to make herself at home and have a look around if she wanted. He was going to take a shower before he changed. "I must smell pretty ripe after that hard run."

"Go right ahead." Rhea smiled at him. On an impulse he kissed her again, and this time it was more of a lingering, promising embrace that left Rhea a little dizzy. He did smell of sweat and she shooed him off before the excitement of being alone with him overwhelmed them both.

Rhea wandered from room to room, enchanted with the

luxurious furniture and *objets d'art*. The owners obviously had not spared any cost in furnishing their second home. A panoramic view of the mountains from the living room windows was stunning. She could hear the water gushing from Trey's shower as she toured the bedrooms, peeking into each one. She knew which one was his because of the clothes that were scattered over the floor and the unmade bed. After the water shut off, Rhea wandered back downstairs.

"You hungry?" Trey asked when he joined her a few minutes later. He had put on a clean pair of blue jeans that clung to his long legs and narrow hips. He was pulling on a tan cowboy shirt with blue trim. A few bristly hairs protruded from his chest. His damp hair had been brushed back and as he approached she detected a sweet, spicy fragrance from his aftershave.

Rhea had begun to feel hunger pangs, but right now her libido was stirring. His clean presence stimulated her senses and she had a wild urge to wrap herself up in those strong arms and succumb to another delectable kiss. She managed to control herself as he took her hand and led her out to the truck.

"I know a place that serves buffalo steaks," he said.

"That sounds ... wonderful," Rhea murmured, never having tasted buffalo.

Darkness had all but masked a lingering melon sunset when they walked into The Smokehouse, a dimly lit establishment on the village mall. Its cloudy, bar-like atmosphere reminded Rhea of the Smuggler in Aspen—only here she heard loud rock music playing rather than country western. Trey led her past the bar to the dining room. Bright red tablecloths draped the six or so tables, where only a few people sat. A young man in jeans and a checkered shirt approached.

"How ya doin' tonight?" he grinned.

Rhea figured Trey was a regular customer at this place. The casually dressed *maitre d'* led them to a vacant table, where he lit a match and touched it to a small lump of wax in a glass bowl on the table.

"No big crowd tonight?" Trey asked him.

The *maitre d'* frowned. "Folks are partied out after the long weekend. That was some fireworks display, wouldn't you say?"

"Don't know," replied Trey. "I wasn't here on the Fourth." He winked at Rhea. "I had other things goin' on."

The young man left. Soon a waitress came to take their orders. She knew Trey too, and regarded Rhea with a look of envy. The meal was tasty and Rhea enjoyed her steak, although it was such a large portion she couldn't eat it all. Trey didn't hesitate to clean her plate for her. She pretended not to notice and asked him questions about his job.

"What will you do after the summer?"

"I usually find somethin'," said Trey. "I've got to admit, I've held lots of jobs. The ski school, then lift operator ... I was a taxi driver one year."

"But what would you do if you could do whatever you wanted?"

Trey thought a moment, then smiled. "I'd tell you, but your bein' a lady ..." He patted her hand.

Ignoring his comment, Rhea asked, "Did you go to college?"

Trey wiped his mouth with the checkered napkin. "Sure, I've been to college. One thing I know ... I like workin' outdoors."

Rhea told him of her dream of being a concert pianist and confessed how she had almost given up that dream last summer.

"You mean, you'da married that guy?"

"Yes." She stared down at the glass of water in which the ice had melted.

"That guy must have been a real Chauvinist to make you give up your dream."

Rhea was quick to respond. "Parker was no Chauvinist. It would have been my choice."

"You know, the more I hear you talk about him, the more I think this Parker guy just wasn't suited to you. How'd he die, anyway?"

Rhea's chin tensed up. "He died in a forest fire."

"Wait. I think I remember that." Trey pondered, tapping the plate with his fork. "Yeah, I seem to recall one of those Forest Service fellas dyin' last fall."

He acted so casually, Rhea couldn't bear it. *Why did they have to talk about Parker, anyway?*

More might have been said, but just at that moment some loud masculine voices intruded on them. A collection of Trey's friends had come through the door and spotted them. Rhea recognized one face from the cowboy crowd at the Smuggler. As his friends crowded around them, Trey greeted them and invited them to sit down.

Rhea smiled in a civil manner, but she felt intimidated. Trey's friends looked her over, making her feel like some prize-winning livestock at the county fair. Trey didn't seem to mind, though, and ordered a pitcher of beer.

Some date this is turning out to be, thought Rhea. She moved closer to Trey and he held her hand as if laying claim to her. The beer arrived and Trey's friends wasted no time slurping it and filling a glass for Rhea. A thin, bony-faced man with blond hair and narrow eyes kept darting his eyes back and forth from Trey to Rhea. When he laughed or talked, Rhea saw he had a broken tooth that made him appear haggard. She soon learned his name was Chance and he was one of Trey's best friends.

Another guy, who was constantly sniffing, they called Hamster. When Rhea heard that, she laughed so hard she almost cried. They kept filling her glass with beer. By the time the party began to break up, her vision had grown fuzzy. Soon only Chance remained at the table with Trey and Rhea.

"Say, you're Mona Whitecloud's roommate, aren't you?" Chance asked.

"Yes."

Chance grinned. "I know her."

Rhea stared at the chipped tooth and nodded, not knowing what to say.

"She that black-haired chubby girl you were with?" asked Trey. "The one who chewed me out?"

"Yes."

"I know her," Chance said again, still grinning.

One of the other guys who hadn't left yet overheard. "Yeah, everybody knows Mona," he called from the bar. "MOAN-aaa ... oooh! Get it?"

"Shut up, Smitty, this is the lady's roommate you're makin'

fun of." Trey turned to Rhea and apologized. "They're a bunch of clods. You ready to go?"

Rhea was grateful to get out of that place. She welcomed the cool night air as they walked to the truck. The foul taste of beer was still in her mouth. She had forgotten to take a mint on the way out. At the truck Trey stopped and drew her toward him.

"Sorry about my friends bargin' in like that," said Trey. "For a while there, I actually thought you were enjoyin' yourself."

Rhea felt secure in his embrace. "What is wrong with your friend Hamster?" she asked.

"Why? What about him?"

"His nose. He sniffs constantly."

Trey laughed. "Oh, that. Probably cocaine."

Rhea stared at Trey's face in the dark. "Do you ...?" she started to ask.

" 'Course not, honeybabe!" He leaned over and kissed her, then drew back. "You're not into that way of life, are ya?"

"No!"

"I didn't think so." Then he smiled. "You really didn't like my friends, did you?"

"Oh, they're ... probably all right."

Trey drew her closer to him. "Don't mind my friends. They don't matter." Then he added, "*You* matter."

Rhea closed her eyes and opened her lips to him. She felt herself sinking within his strong embrace. Sparks exploded everywhere inside of her. In her mind she heard the words *I love him ... I really love him ...*

They got into the truck and Trey turned the key to start the engine. Rhea knew what was coming next. He was going to ask, "Your place or mine?" The evening could end no other way, especially after their last night together up at Snowmass Lake. She let him kiss her again and welcomed the warm mouth that met hers. Prickles of delight surged throughout her and she longed for him to fondle her as he had the other night.

Gently Trey broke away and sighed. "Much as I hate to break this to you, I have to take you home now. John and I've got that horse trip tomorrow and I have to get up before dawn."

Rhea leaned her head against him once they were headed down Snowmelt Road. She knew she should be relieved that they weren't going back to his house. She was so groggy from the beer ... and she had these crazy ideas about *love* inside her head.

She relaxed as the truck bumped over the road and her mind went back to last summer.

Mona had been excited to hear about Rhea's engagement to Parker. She agreed to be Rhea's maid of honor. "Are you getting married on a mountain top?" she had asked. "Or better yet, Maroon Lake will be perfect the end of September."

"No, we're getting married in a church," Rhea replied. "The Prince of Peace Chapel, we hope. Parker wants it there."

"Oh, is he religious or something?"

"Does he have to be?" Rhea laughed. "Oh Mona, I'm so happy. I've never been this happy in my entire life."

"Marriage will suit you. You're going to be a lovely bride."

Parker broke the news at the Forest Service. The next week when Rhea came in for her volunteer work, the women fell all over her with their congratulations and excitement.

"How did you do it?" asked Janet. "How did you ever manage to break through that hard shell of his?"

Practical Marie suggested throwing a bridal shower and asked Rhea for a date that was convenient. Rhea begged them not to go to any fuss over her.

"There goes another eligible bachelor," one of the seasonals bemoaned.

"Don't exaggerate," said Janet. "Parker never acted very eligible around any of us."

"But he's still the best catch around," somebody else added.

Rhea called her parents with the news. They sounded shocked at first to learn of her plans, particularly when she told them how soon they would occur. But then Rhea told them what Parker was like and how much in love they were. By the end of the conversation, her mother was bubbling with wedding ideas and the prospect of doing all she could to help. Her father was looking forward to meeting "the young man."

"But I won't believe he's good enough for my daughter until I meet him face to face," said her father. "A federal employee, eh? Well, at least he ought to be able to provide for you."

"Oh Dad, you'll like Parker, I just know it. And Mom ... are you still on the line?"

"I'm still here, dear."

"Mom, you'll be here, won't you?"

"Of course. I'll make the air reservations first thing in the morning."

"We're here. Time to wake up." Trey nudged Rhea and she sat up, aware that they had arrived at her apartment building. The truck idled along the side of the street.

"I wasn't asleep," she said. Thoughts from last summer still lingered as she recalled the many times Parker had brought her home, just like Trey had now.

"What's wrong?" he asked.

"Nothing," said Rhea. "I was just ... thinking ..."

He put his arms around her and kissed her above the ear. "Daydreaming?"

Rhea didn't want to reveal her private thoughts. She moved her head and let him kiss her, but her mind still swarmed with memories of Parker.

"Somethin's troubling you," said Trey. "You okay?"

"I'm fine," she said.

Trey sighed impatiently. "Can't you *forget* him?"

"No." Rhea withdrew from his embrace. "I can't."

"I want to make you forget him," said Trey. "I can, you know."

"We were to be married." Rhea's voice cracked on the word.

"So what?"

It stung and Rhea began to cry. "I still love Parker. It still hurts. Don't you understand?"

A silence ensued and then Trey got out of the truck to help her out. "Somehow I didn't plan on the evenin' endin' this way," he grumbled. He opened her door and she stepped out.

"You don't have to walk me to the door," she uttered.

"Well, I aim to make you forget him. You hear me?" Next he grabbed her and kissed her hard, then released her. "One way or another, Rhea, I'll make you forget that guy."

Rhea stood in a daze as Trey walked around the truck, got in, and drove off into the night.

10

*T*he week passed quickly with practice and music classes taking up Rhea's time. To keep up she had to delve into her work with fervor. She forced Trey Michaels from her thoughts every time her mind began to wander. It helped that he was away, for it made it easier to concentrate on those things she felt she had neglected.

Late Thursday afternoon Rhea bought an *Aspen Times* and, when she got home, searched through the help wanted section of the classified ads. Mona was getting ready to go to work and stuck her head in the door of Rhea's bedroom.

"Anything in the ads this week?"

"I'm looking." Rhea's eyes moved down the column, picking out the first few words of each ad.

"AGGRESSIVE, PROFITABLE REAL ESTATE COMPANY SEEKS ...

"JOBS OVERSEAS ...

"APPLICATIONS NOW BEING TAKEN FOR STATION MANAGER ...

"PHOTO LAB TECHNICIAN ...

"GOVERNESS, FULL TIME ...

"SWITCHBOARD OPERATOR ...

"FULL-TIME EXECUTIVE SECRETARY ...

"PART-TIME DENTAL ASSISTANT, EXPERIENCE NECESSARY ...

"FULL CHARGE BOOKKEEPER ...

"WAITRESS ...

"MAIDS, FLEXIBLE HOURS ...

"RELIABLE BABY SITTER ..."

Rhea sighed, turning the page. It was the same thing as last week. Then she stopped as the word PIANIST caught her eye. The ad said, "Pianist wanted for rehearsals. Temporary employment. Excellent pay. Call Mrs. Whitney, Aspen Ballet Company."

When Rhea showed Mona the ad, her roommate said, "That must be Mark Whitney's wife. He's the artistic director at Aspen Ballet. There was a big article in last week's *Times* about them."

"I wonder what the hours are like," mused Rhea.

"Why don't you call?" urged Mona.

"They probably need someone in the morning. I have most of my classes in the morning."

"Well, you won't know unless you call."

Rhea called the number, but Mrs. Whitney was not available, so she left a message with her name and number.

"Well?" asked Mona after Rhea hung up.

"She'll get back to me," said Rhea. "I've heard that one before."

"Oh, cheer up. Something's got to come along."

Rhea collapsed on the couch. "What am I going to do if it doesn't? I've got five dollars and twenty-eight cents in my checking account. You've been buying all of the food lately, and I haven't even paid you the rent."

"Don't worry about it, Rhea. I'm not going to turn you out on the street. By the way, did you ever call your parents back?"

Rhea shook her head. A wave of guilt surfaced. "I'm too poor to make a long distance call."

"For heaven's sake, Rhea!"

"Besides, I just know they'll try to talk me into coming home."

"Why?"

"They think I'm wasting away. They think I don't belong out here."

"That's ridiculous."

"I don't want to leave Aspen," said Rhea.

"You mean, you don't want to leave Parker."

Rhea looked up in surprise. Mona could be so perceptive at times. Then she sighed. "But if I don't start earning some money soon, I won't be able to afford the high cost of living here."

"Relax. Mrs. Whitney will probably call you. Why don't you go jog or something? Take your mind off it. I've got to get to work."

After Mona left, Rhea decided that a run would help her feel better. She changed into her shorts and rode her bike down to the river. She hadn't run since the day she had last seen Trey.

I'm getting lax, she told herself as she locked up her bike. As she warmed up before her run, Rhea thought of Trey and realized she missed him. In fact, she missed him a lot. How pleasant it had been to run the whole three miles with him last week. It was good having him at her side, keeping up with her pace and enjoying it as much as she did.

"Did you truly enjoy yourself?" A voice disrupted her recollection. Parker was standing in front of her, waiting for an answer.

Rhea stood up and did some waist bends. She feigned innocence. "Oh hi, Parker ... I wasn't sure you'd be running today."

"And why would you think that, Rhea?"

"After you didn't finish the race ... I thought ..."

Parker shrugged good-naturedly. *"Oh well, you win some, you lose some. Maybe it just wasn't my day."*

They began to jog side by side, but Rhea was disturbed by Parker's presence. There was a tenseness between them. She *could* make him go away ...

"I thought we'd have a discussion while we run," said Parker.

"Oh?" Rhea wondered if Parker was jealous.

"It's only natural you are attracted to other men." Parker paused, then said, *"I can't expect to hold onto you like this. But I feel I must tell you, Rhea. This guy is destined to hurt you."*

For a few moments they jogged in silence. Rhea couldn't understand how he could possibly know these things. "Why are you telling me this?"

"Trust me, Rhea. Don't see Trey anymore. He'll hurt you because of the kind of man he is."

"Trey has been good to me so far," Rhea challenged. "And ... and ... aren't you forgetting? You hurt me, too, Parker. You hurt me deeply. Why did you have to *die?*"

He had no answer to this. Rhea ran on without looking at him. Toward the end of the run she noticed Parker had disappeared. But she felt no comfort in the fact that she had told him off. She slowed to a walk. Maybe there was truth in what Parker said. He was concerned for her well-being and he did exist on another earth plane, didn't he? Perhaps he could know about things that the living had to find out in their own way. How was she to know if this thing between herself and Trey Michaels was not just a trivial affair in Trey's eyes?

As she walked her bicycle uphill, she thought back to another discussion—one she and Parker had when he was alive. They were enjoying an evening at his house last summer when he abruptly turned her away during another one of their necking sessions.

"Parker, why did we stop?" asked Rhea. "We're practically man and wife."

"Why can't you be patient, Rhea? Our wedding night isn't that far away."

"Parker, I don't want to wait till our wedding night to make love. We've got to talk about this."

"Talk about what?"

"How you feel … about sex."

He was silent.

"Why do we always have to stop?" she persisted.

They lay together on the couch and he stroked her hair. "I care about you too much," he said.

"But if you care about me, make love to me! What is your hangup?"

He wouldn't give her any satisfaction. Finally she gave up trying to talk about that aspect of their relationship. She didn't want to cause a problem. Besides, their wedding night was only a couple of weeks away.

The woman from the ballet company called Rhea after she got home from jogging. They set up an appointment to meet the next day. "But the job is only temporary, you realize," said Mrs. Whitney.

"I know." After Rhea hung up, she smiled. There was hope. She wouldn't have to rely on Mona's charity much longer if things worked out. She spent the rest of the evening practicing.

The next morning Rhea's session with her piano instructor went well. She was delighted when Ms. Bent told her to bring some of Debussy's music to work on. Later, when she stepped onto the bus to take her back to Aspen, Rhea saw Jerome Hodges and sat down next to him.

"Hello, Jerome. How are you?"

Jerome cleared his throat. "Excuse me. I'm still recovering from last weekend." He drew out a large white handkerchief and blew his nose. "Nothing worse than a lousy cold in mid-July."

"That's too bad," said Rhea. "Are you still planning on going to the Tent concert with me tomorrow?"

"I think I'll have to pass on that." Jerome dug into a pants pocket and produced a ticket. "Here. Why don't you see if your friend, the outfitter, can go with you?"

"Trey's gone until next week."

"Well, take it anyway. You should be able to find somebody to go with you."

Rhea accepted the ticket. "Thanks. By the way, do you ever see Betsy Lawrence?"

Jerome kept a straight face. "Nope. Don't really care to one way or the other." He put his handkerchief away. "The Lawrences asked about you. They said to say hello."

Rhea smiled, remembering how Professor Lawrence had peeked out the flap of the tent when Trey had kissed her. At least he had kept quiet about it. The Lawrences were good people. Too bad they had to put up with a daughter like Betsy.

Rhea was offered the piano accompaniment job at the Aspen Ballet. Mrs. Whitney already knew about her credentials through the Music School. The regular accompanist had taken a personal leave, but was supposed to return in two weeks.

"We want you to start Monday," Mrs. Whitney told Rhea.

"That's fine." Rhea left, happy that it had worked out with the hours and that the pay was acceptable. But the job was only for two weeks. That meant that soon she would be right back where she started.

Saturday afternoon Rhea was busy with a reading assignment when Trey telephoned. At the sound of his voice she grew excited. "Trey! I thought you'd be gone till next week."

"I need to see you, Rhea."

Why did he sound serious? Was something wrong? Then she remembered Parker's words on the Rio Grande Trail, *"This guy is destined to hurt you ..."*

"Are you still there?"

"Yes," Rhea replied.

"Mind if I come over?"

Rhea explained that she had a concert to attend in an hour and suggested meeting him afterwards.

"I need to talk to you before then. How about if I take you to that concert?"

As she hung up Rhea was relieved, even though Parker's words still echoed in her mind, *"Don't see Trey anymore ..."* She hadn't been able to find anyone to go to the concert with her and she still had Jerome's ticket.

Rhea stood outside her apartment, waiting for Trey. He was late and she was worried they'd get to the concert after it had started. She hated to be late for anything. Then she saw the blue truck draw up along the curb. She hurried over and hopped in, not waiting for him to get out first.

"Hello," Trey said cheerfully. "Hope I didn't keep you waiting."

"We can still make it if you burn rubber," Rhea remarked.

"Sorry." Trey drove on back streets toward the Tent. "But I figured you'd prefer me to shower and shave first."

Rhea said nothing. In a few minutes Trey drove into the parking lot, which was almost full. A few stragglers were still heading for the ticket booth, she noticed. She tried the door handle, but it was stuck again.

"What's your hurry?" Trey reached over and laid his hand on her arm. "Don't I even get a kiss? I haven't seen you in days."

Rhea turned to him. Her impatience ebbed as she caught the twinkle in his eye. She dutifully bent toward him. His lips touched hers and she drew back immediately. "We'll have to run," she said and tried the door handle again.

Trey edged closer to her. "Why don't we just skip the concert?"

"Trey!" Rhea grew annoyed.

He sighed and got out of the truck to let her out. "All right, if it's that important to you."

"It is."

They practically ran up the path to the Tent. When they got inside, they slid into seats just moments before the first performance began.

"See? We made it," Trey whispered and squeezed her hand.

"Shh." Rhea sat rigid and attentive. The artist on stage was one of her teachers from last summer and she wanted to concentrate on the music. She was aware of Trey's fingers playing inside hers. His presence was a distraction and she finally withdrew her hand from his. Several minutes later, after the music ended and the applause followed, Rhea noticed Trey again and smiled at him.

Halfway through the second performance, Rhea caught Trey glancing at his watch. He looked totally bored and she felt sorry that she had made him come. During the intermission she asked him if he wanted to leave.

"Are you sure?" he responded. "You seem to be enjoying it."

"But I can see you're not."

He scratched his head and shrugged.

Rhea sighed. "Let's go."

On the way back to her apartment, they were silent like before. Rhea sensed something was on Trey's mind. After missing him all week, she had looked forward to seeing him again and somehow her expectations were falling short.

When Rhea stepped out of the truck, she noticed a suitcase in the back. "Are you going somewhere?" she asked.

Trey took her arm and led her toward the building. " 'Fraid so. That's why I had to see you."

"Oh? Where do you have to go?" Rhea inserted the key and unlocked the door.

He sighed. "I've got to be in Texas tonight."

"Texas? Is it your family? I hope nothing is wrong."

"Nothin' I can't handle. Just some personal business."

"How long will you be gone?"

"Don't rightly know."

"A few days? A week?"

"Can't say."

Rhea didn't want him to go away even for a few days. He had just gotten back after being away a week.

"I hope not that long," Trey added.

"You don't want to tell me anything about it, do you?"

Trey winced. "Well, it does have something to do with a relative." He smiled then and put his arms around her. "But it's nothin' for you to worry your pretty head about, little lady."

When he kissed her, it was like she had been swept away by a gust of wind. He drew her tight and his lips explored hers, forcing her mouth open. Rhea's mind swam with sensations and body awareness. If only he didn't have to leave for Texas.

Before she even realized what was happening, Trey had managed to get her onto the couch. She couldn't resist. She was a slave to his caresses. Time had little meaning. There was just Trey and herself. Yet some voice in the back of her mind began to intrude. She didn't want to hear it. She wanted only to surrender to the man who wanted her and whose touch was so pleasing.

"*Hurt you ... hurt you,*" the voice said.

Rhea tensed up and Trey seemed to know immediately that something was wrong. He moved aside and stared at her curiously. "What's wrong?" he whispered.

"You ... you'll hurt me," Rhea murmured. She hadn't meant to say it, actually. The words were echoes of the voice in her head —Parker's voice.

Trey stroked her cheek. "I'd never hurt you, darlin'."

Rhea opened her mouth to speak, but nothing came out.

Trey studied her intently. "Hey, you're not ... I mean, you've made love before, haven't you?"

Rhea sat up. So *that* was it. He thought she was easy.

"No, forget I asked," said Trey. "Of course you and him had

to. I mean, you were engaged to the guy."

Rhea forced herself to her feet. She shook her hair. "Parker was right." Anger swelled from within.

Trey appeared startled. "Huh? Did I miss something?"

"I think you should leave," said Rhea, not looking at him. "I'm not that kind of girl."

Trey didn't move. "I know that," he replied calmly. "But I don't understand what you're talkin' about. Parker's right? What in tarnation is Parker right about? What are you talkin' about?"

Rhea almost felt dizzy. "He said you'd hurt me."

"What?" Trey stood up next to her. "Who said that?"

"Parker."

"When?"

Suddenly the words tumbled out of Rhea's mouth. She had no control. "On the Rio Grande Trail. He ... he runs with me. We ... we talk. He said ..." She walked across the room to pick up one of Parker's pictures. His face smiled back at her as if to say, *"I'm glad you told him."*

Rhea expected Trey to make a sarcastic comment or laugh. Certainly by now he must think she was crazy. Now that she had revealed her terrible secret, what would he do? Probably walk out, never to return.

Trey came over to stand behind her. He looked over her shoulder at the photograph, but he wasn't laughing. "So you actually talk to this guy?"

Rhea clutched the picture to her breast. There was no sense trying to deny any of it. "Sometimes," she said. When he didn't answer right away, she said, "You don't believe me, do you?"

"What, that you talk to a dead guy?"

"His body is dead, Trey. His spirit is still alive."

Trey cleared his throat. "Let me ask you something," he said.

Rhea turned to look at him. He had a straight face. His reaction was a little unexpected.

"I want you to tell me again, Rhea. When did Parker die, and where?"

Rhea was confused. This was a sick game.

"You said it was a forest fire. Where was this forest fire, Rhea?"

"Somewhere near Rifle," she said. "It was on BLM land."

"BLM ... you mean Bureau of Land Management? Do you know where exactly?"

"No." She admitted she knew very little facts regarding Parker's death.

"Hmm ... maybe he's not dead."

Now it was Rhea's turn to look startled. "Why would you even ask me such a thing?" she demanded.

"I want to know the facts," said Trey. "And I don't think you know them all. I don't think you've accepted Parker's death."

Rhea drew in a breath, struggling to hold back tears. "Why are you tormenting me?" She felt fire in her cheeks. "You *do* want to hurt me!"

"No ... Rhea, please."

"Go on, get out!" she cried. "Go back to Texas. Just leave me alone!"

"Okay, I'm going." Trey headed for the door.

Rhea waited to hear the door slam, but when it didn't, she glanced over to see him still standing there. The compassion on his face and the sadness in his brown eyes were genuine. Even though she was angry, he had not made fun of her when she told him about Parker.

Before he could turn around and leave, a compulsion swept over Rhea. She dashed over to him and fell into his arms. She loved Trey Michaels and began mumbling apologies and wetting his shirt with her silent tears.

"Don't go," she pleaded.

Trey held her tight. "I have to."

"Why?" she asked.

"I have a plane to catch in Denver," he said, caressing her. "I'll try not to be gone long. I promise that much." When he kissed her, it was a long, binding embrace, filled with a promise. When Rhea opened her eyes she was surprised at the moisture in his eyes as he released her and hurried out the door. There was no doubt about it. She knew she was in love with Trey Michaels, and she'd be counting the days till his return.

11

*O*ne week had passed since Rhea started working for the ballet school. She came home and dropped her backpack onto the couch. Mona had the evening off and had put on a colorful summer dress.

"Let's splurge and eat out tonight," said Mona.

Rhea thought about it a moment, then agreed. "But only if you let me pay for my own meal."

"Okay."

Rhea noticed Mona's colorful dress made her plump figure more pronounced. For some reason her roommate had a glow about her. "Why are you all dolled up on your night off?" she asked.

"No special reason. Come on, let's go. I'm starved."

"Where are we going?"

"If I tell you, you'll want to stay home," said Mona.

"Not The Lucky Find!"

Mona frowned. "Would I be that cruel?"

"Where, then?"

"I've got a yen for Mexican tonight."

Rhea relaxed. "Oh, so we're going to El Cid's?"

"Not exactly."

Rhea soon discovered Mona had the Smuggler Bar in mind. But when they walked down the concrete steps, she didn't protest. For some reason the dark little establishment no longer intimidated her. A warm feeling filled her as she thought of Trey and the first day she had met him.

"Let's sit near the door," said Mona.

They found a booth and sat down. Few people were in the

Smuggler tonight, Rhea noticed, but smoke still hung in a cloud over the bar area. "At least we can make a quick getaway if we have to," Rhea chuckled.

"You ought to be fond of this place," said Mona. "After all, this is where you met Trey."

Rhea didn't comment as the waitress handed them menus, then walked away.

Mona's eyes roved as if she were looking for someone in particular. "Where did you say Trey went, anyway?"

"Texas."

"How long is he going to be gone?"

"He didn't know."

"Don't you miss him?"

"I suppose." Rhea was scanning the menu when some guys walked in and brushed against their table. She looked up and recognized one of them as Trey's haggard-looking friend with the chipped front tooth.

Mona grabbed his leg as he passed. "Hello, turkey."

Chance looked surprised. "Mona! How you doin'?"

"Rhea, I want you to meet Chance Kelley—an old friend," said Mona.

Chance nodded at Rhea in greeting. "We already met," he said.

Rhea noticed the other guys had moved to the bar. Chance sat down next to Mona and the two of them began nudging each other and laughing. Rhea wondered if Mona had planned the meeting. She was beginning to feel like a fifth wheel.

"Let's get a pitcher," Chance said when the waitress returned.

"Rhea, will you drink with us?" asked Mona.

Rhea wrinkled up her nose. "I'll just have a glass of wine," she told the waitress, then ordered an enchilada and a salad.

"Three burritos," Chance told the girl.

The waitress wrote down the order and started to walk away, but Chance called out, "Wait! You forgot Mona."

"Oh, I thought ..." The waitress gaped at Chance. "You're going to eat three whole burritos yourself?"

Mona laughed. "Make that four burritos. One's for me."

Rhea watched the interaction between the two. Obviously Mona had a thing for Trey's friend. She wondered how Mona felt about kissing somebody with a broken tooth. She sipped her water and stared toward the smoky bar. The flirtations going on across from her faded as the mention of burritos brought back a memory from last summer.

Since knowing Parker, Rhea had become fond of Mexican food. Parker, having grown up in California, had been raised on it. They were making a batch of burritos over at his house the evening Parker got the call about the forest fire. He grated the cheese while she stood over the stove and stirred the refried beans. The phone rang and Parker went to answer it.

Rhea could tell by the conversation that Parker was talking to Bill Marshall, the district ranger. When Parker hung up, she detected a familiar glow in his expression. "Another fire?" she asked.

"The BLM started a controlled burn down near Rifle," said Parker. "They were playing with their new flame thrower and the fire got out of control."

"What were they doing having a controlled burn at this time of year?"

"They do as they please," Parker muttered. "I have to leave right away." He came over and put his arms around her waist. "You can start rolling the tortillas now. Remember how I showed you?"

"Parker, you've got time to eat first, don't you?"

"Probably not. I'd better go round up my fire pack." He kissed her cheekbone. "Why don't you drive my car home?"

Rhea turned the burner off and spun around. "How long will you be gone this time?" she asked.

Parker shrugged. "Probably just overnight. Two or three days at the most." He kissed her gently on the lips and smiled. "Don't worry about me. I don't think it's anything serious."

"Did Bill say that?"

Parker left the kitchen to get his pack and change into fire-fighting clothes. "Just think of it as extra money to spend on our honeymoon," he called from the bedroom.

Disappointed that their evening was being cut short, Rhea frowned. By the time she finished wrapping the burritos, Parker was ready to head over to the office, where he was meeting the rest of the fire crew. Although he was anxious to get going, he accepted the napkin-wrapped burrito she handed him as he stepped out the door.

"Please be careful," she told him.

Parker stopped and set down his pack, then turned and came back. "I almost forgot something," he said as he stood over her.

Rhea ignored the old smoke smell from the yellow firefighting uniform as Parker collected her in his arms and kissed her long and hard. It roused her from her worries and invoked longings hard to control. As she lingered in his arms, she realized that when he returned, it would be only a week until she could be totally his.

"You'll come back soon?" she asked.

"I can't bear to be away from you too long," he replied.

"Don't keep me waiting at the altar," she teased.

Parker messed up her hair and grinned. "See you in a day or two."

"I love you!" she called out. He waved back before he disappeared through the shortcut in the woods.

The waitress set the plate down in front of her. Rhea blinked from the steam as she returned to the present. She hadn't noticed the glass of wine the waitress had already brought. She reached for it and took a sip, then set it down as Mona and Chance dug into their burritos.

"Boy, oh boy," exclaimed Chance. "Here, Mona, try some."

"I've got my own, you turd."

Chance stuffed his paper napkin over his collar and picked up his fork. Then he caught Rhea staring at him. "You want some?"

"No, thank you."

"She's awful quiet, ain't she?" Chance asked Mona.

"Well, right now she is, but I'm sure it's only because you've struck her by your charm."

Rhea took a bite of her enchilada, not paying any attention. What Mona saw in Chance Kelley was beyond her imagination.

"Or maybe it's because she's lonely," prompted Chance. He looked around. "I got a friend who might cheer you up."

Mona slapped his wrist. "Turn around and eat, you big lug. Rhea's not interested in any of your friends."

Chance stuffed his mouth, chewed a bit, then swallowed. After a long gulp from his beer glass, he said, "I seen you with Trey, though. 'Course he's off to Texas to see his girlfriend and all. Who knows, he might never come back."

Rhea's enchilada suddenly tasted like rubber. What was Chance talking about?

"Stop kidding around," Mona chided him. "Of course Trey's coming back. Isn't he, Rhea?"

Rhea couldn't reply with her mouth full.

Chance took a large bite and talked while he chewed. "What's-Her-Face sent him a ticket and said, 'Come on out for a good time.' I reckon he'll stay till she's tired of him. Heck, she's got the bucks."

Mona's black eyes flashed in anger. "I ought to rap you on the side of the head!" she told Chance.

Rhea tried to keep her cool, but her insides were revolting. Chance had to be lying. It couldn't be true. Trey Michaels wouldn't have done a thing like that. *She* was his girlfriend, wasn't she?

"Did I say something wrong?" Chance stared at Rhea.

"You idiot," Mona grumbled.

Rhea got up from the table and found her way to the bathroom. She couldn't stand another minute at that table. She locked herself up in a stall and stood there as her eyes burned with indignation. *Please, God*, she pleaded, *don't let it be true.* Yet, Chance was Trey's friend—one of his closest friends, he had said—and he must know why Trey had gone to Texas. If it was true—if Trey had gone to see a woman—then of course he would have kept this from her.

Chance's words burned over and over in her head ... "Off to Texas to see his girlfriend ... she sent him a ticket ... he'll stay till she's tired of him ..."

The outer door swung open. "Rhea?" Mona called in. "You okay?"

Rhea composed herself, but said in a tight voice, "I'm fine."

"Chance wants to apologize for what he said."

Rhea didn't see what good it would do for Chance to apologize. What had been said was said. The damage was done and the truth was out. She felt used. All week she had surrendered to the fact that she was in love with Trey Michaels. Now to find out he was off on a pleasure trip, keeping company with some Texas tart ...

"Mona, I'm going home," said Rhea. She flushed the toilet and emerged from the stall and washed her hands. She ripped a paper towel off the spool, wadded it up and threw it away.

"Oh Rhea, I know how you must feel."

"It's not likely," said Rhea. She sighed. "It's my fault, actually. I was just fooling myself all along. Well, I'll tell you one thing. I'll never make that mistake again." She marched out of the restroom and grabbed her pack on the way out. Chance was too busy hogging down his burritos to pay much attention.

Rhea hurried home to the apartment, feeling humiliated and betrayed. How she wished she never had to see Trey Michaels' miserable face again.

Mrs. Whitney left Rhea's paycheck for her as prearranged. Now that her two-week stint with the ballet company had ended, Rhea regretted seeing the job end. She had gotten used to playing for the rehearsals and had mastered the music. But the other accompanist was back in town. Rhea would have to find another means of coming up with August's rent money. And she only had a week to do it.

As she walked downtown toward the bank with the pay envelope tucked in her pack, Rhea thought back over the week. Classes and piano practice kept her busy. She had hardly seen nor spoken with Mona. After what Chance had said in the Smuggler about Trey, Rhea made up her mind to drive him out of her thoughts by becoming totally involved with her music. So far, she had to admit, it was working. But with the weekend ahead of her—and once again facing no job—Rhea began to give in to depression.

Standing in line at the bank, she was startled out of her self-pity when she noticed Mr. Cox from The Lucky Find. His gut stuck out more than usual, she noticed, as he waited, kind of slumped over in the next line. She prayed he wouldn't see her, but as she stared straight ahead, she could already feel his penetrating eyes falling on her. She refused to look in his direction. Disgusting recollections surfaced and she busied herself by pretending to search for a pen in her pack. The person ahead of Rhea certainly seemed to be taking up enough time at the teller window. She glanced up and saw Mr. Cox stepping up to the next window.

Rhea was still waiting her turn when the restaurant manager finished his business and turned around. It was too late. He had seen her watching him. He came over and greeted her. "Well, well, if it isn't Miss Sinclair."

Rhea didn't smile. "It is."

"And how are you faring in this economically inflated town? Playing the piano over at Gustav's, perhaps?" Although he was acting polite, to Rhea it came across as spiteful mockery.

"No," she replied. She didn't want to reveal that she was still unemployed.

Mr. Cox slowly shook his head, his narrow eyes probing her bare shoulders. "Too bad." He started to walk away, then swung around. "I could still use someone of your caliber at my piano bar, if you're interested."

Rhea tensed up. The man ahead of her was leaving. "I don't think I am, but thank you just the same."

"Very well. But if you should change your mind ..." Mr. Cox shrugged as he walked away. "I like your style."

Rhea stepped up to the window and presented her check. She breathed a sigh of relief as she saw Mr. Cox go out the door. A chill caused her to shudder. The man was a creep. She would never go back and work for him.

When she got home, she found a note from Mona that said she would be gone for the weekend. She was going off with Chance on his motorcycle to Telluride. As much as Rhea was glad Mona had someone, she still wondered what her roommate saw in Chance Kelley.

"Stop! Start again," directed Caroline Bent from across the room.

Rhea dropped her hands and looked around. "You mean from the beginning?"

"Yes, from the beginning." The music teacher's voice was firm but patient.

Rhea flipped back through the pages, surprised that Ms. Bent had allowed her to get almost halfway through the piece. She found C-sharp and slowly started into Debussy's *L'Apres-Midi d'un Faune*. Before she had finished the first rippling glissando, Ms. Bent stopped her again.

"No! no! You aren't putting enough mood into it."

Rhea sighed. "It's no use."

Ms. Bent motioned Rhea aside, then sat down and made the broken chords come alive in the magical, mystical tones Rhea knew so well. "Now, you make it sound the same."

Rhea resumed her place, but this time she flubbed up. "Darn," she hissed.

"Relax!"

"I can't!"

"You are angry."

Rhea said nothing.

"You cannot perform this delicate piece of music when there is fire in your heart," said the instructor. "You must let out what is eating you."

Rhea stared at the black and white keys. She knew Ms. Bent was right. She couldn't supply the proper emotion for the piece, and no matter how much she tried to drown her feelings about Trey through the music, the hurt and the anger kept surfacing.

"We will quit class early today," said Ms. Bent. "But before you go, I want you to tell me what it is that troubles you."

Rhea closed her book and gathered up her other music. "I'll be all right," she said.

"I think it is like before," said Ms. Bent. "You have a man on your mind."

Rhea did not want to discuss Trey Michaels, especially with someone like Caroline Bent. The music instructor seemed to sense her reluctance.

"Young girls can be so sensitive, and men so unfeeling," said Ms. Bent.

"I'm not a young girl," said Rhea, "I'm almost thirty years old."

This response brought a smile to the older woman's tight face. "Ah, almost thirty, and married to your music, no doubt. No room for a man in your life, I take it." She sighed. "You are right, of course. No man is worth it."

Rhea left, thinking perhaps Ms. Bent was right. No man was worth all this misery. So far the men in her life had caused her only pain—especially Trey. She had fallen in love with him, only to have him go off to Texas to play gigolo to some rich woman.

A couple of weeks later, Rhea was strolling across the Music School campus between classes. She planned on finding a grassy spot near the pond to sit and read. Suddenly, she saw Elizabeth Lawrence walking toward her.

"Hello, Mrs. Lawrence," Rhea called out.

"Rhea! You're just the person I wanted to talk to."

"Oh?" Rhea shaded her eyes from the noon sun.

"Yes. Jerome mentioned you may be in need of a job."

"Do you know of anything?"

"Arthur is absolutely snowed under with work," said Elizabeth. "He needs someone to copy over his manuscripts. When Jerome mentioned your name, we both knew you would be perfect for the job."

"Manuscripts?" Rhea made a face. "I'm afraid my typing skills are a bit rusty. To be quite honest, I'm a terrible typist."

Elizabeth laughed. "Oh no, Rhea, these are his musical compositions. Jerome said you had very legible handwriting."

Rhea sighed in relief. "Copying music. That's different. When would you like me to start?"

Elizabeth Lawrence invited Rhea to have dinner at their condominium that evening, so they could discuss hours and pay.

Rhea's spirits soared as she watched the vocal instructor walk away. She had been wondering what she was going to do. Her financial worries had been preying on her mind and she had even contemplated going back to The Lucky Find. But now she could wipe that loathsome thought out of her head.

Rhea went to work for Arthur Lawrence the next day. The Lawrences were renting a luxury condominium in Aspen for the summer and preferred her to work in their home. She was glad to get out of her stuffy apartment, especially with an August heat wave making the afternoons and evenings sheer misery. The professor had a number of compositions he needed transposed and copied. Rhea came in to work on them whenever she was free.

Lately most her time was free. She was staying ahead in her classes, which she commended herself for, yet she was losing her enthusiasm as the days passed. She did what was expected of her and no more. Ms. Bent continued to coach her on Debussy's prelude and had finally stopped nagging her about the "man in her life."

"It's the way creative and artistic people must endure," Ms. Bent told her before she quit lecturing on the subject. "We feel things a lot deeper than most people, which makes us more vulnerable to heartache."

At home Rhea became more restless and dissatisfied. Mona was gone almost all the time now that she was seeing Chance on a regular basis. Rhea couldn't forget how Parker had warned her about Trey. In a way she was grateful to Parker for trying to tell her. He had said Trey would hurt her—and he had. But she also regretted telling Trey about Parker's warning. Why hadn't she kept her mouth shut? How could she expect anyone—especially Trey—to understand something like that?

One evening, while she was jogging just before dusk, Parker appeared at her side without warning. She had not allowed him to run with her for several days, but tonight she surrendered. It had grown increasingly difficult to push him away. Loneliness finally had gotten the better of her.

"*I take it you haven't heard from our friend,*" he began.

Rhea had known he would start in on it. "No," she replied. "I haven't heard from Trey, if that's who you mean."

"How long has he been away?"

"Three weeks ... I think."

"Hmm," said Parker, *"not even a postcard."*

Rhea shook her head. It had actually been thirty-two days since Trey left, but she didn't reveal this to Parker.

"Doesn't that tell you something, Rhea?"

She turned to him. "Should it?"

"Well, it seems clear to me that Trey simply doesn't care about you as much as he led you to believe." Parker's voice was gentle, but it hurt to hear the words. *"I told you Trey would hurt you."*

When she didn't say anything in response, Parker continued.

"You might thank me for warning you. After all, I still care about you."

A side-stitch suddenly gripped Rhea and she slowed down. Parker slowed with her.

"As long as you're on earth," he said, *"I will look after you ... because I love you, Rhea."*

Rhea ducked under a tree and slid down an embankment. She was choked with emotion and tears filled her eyes. A moment later, Parker climbed down beside her. "Hold me, Parker." She began to sob. "I need you to hold me. I need to feel your arms around me ... to touch me ... to kiss me ..."

A sadness crept over Parker's face. *"You know I love you."*

"Then hold me!"

"I ... can't." He reached for her, but he could not touch her.

Rhea saw him fade away. She sank to her knees in despair and cried.

12

*W*ith the summer drawing to an end, Jerome became Rhea's saving grace. They hung out together on campus and often shared meals. They attended concerts and master classes together. Jerome never asked Rhea about Trey.

Rhea didn't particularly enjoy hanging around Jerome's circle of friends. They were likable enough, but most of them were egotistical. They often put down the locals in Aspen. Such gossip didn't appeal to Rhea. Inside she continued to feel self-pity.

She didn't want to admit it, but she missed Trey and the attention he had given her. Somehow he had been able to make her feel special again. He had aroused the womanly instincts she had buried too quickly after losing Parker. A week or two ago she had still been angry and upset, but time had melted the coldness in her heart. Now she missed him and longed to be held in his arms.

One afternoon in mid-August, while Rhea practiced for her last piano session with Caroline Bent, a delivery person came to the door with a package of seven red roses. Addressed to Rhea, the note read: "I've missed you. Love, Trey."

"Who did you get flowers from?" asked Mona when she walked into the room.

Rhea sniffed the roses and smiled. She found an empty bottle and began sticking the roses into it. "Who do you think?"

"Trey?"

"Yes." Rhea drew in the luscious perfume of the delicate red petals.

"Well, he certainly has taste," said Mona.

Rhea sighed. "But why haven't I heard from him before this?"

She stopped and frowned as she remembered Chance's words in the restaurant. She knew Mona was thinking the same thing.

"Oh, what does it matter?" Mona shrugged. "I wish somebody would send me flowers once."

"Are you still going out with Chance?" Rhea wondered.

"Uh-huh." Mona stood in front of the mirror and gathered her dark straight hair into a ponytail.

Rhea carried the roses into the kitchen for water. The doorbell rang while she filled the bottle.

"I'll get it," called out Mona. "Chance said he might drop by before I go to work."

Rhea brought the bottle of flowers back into the living room, but stopped short. Trey stood at the door. Mona had left the room.

"Hello, pretty lady." He was dressed in a clean western shirt and new blue jeans. Rhea could see that he had gotten his hair cut. The brown scraggly pieces no longer dangled over his ears, and his mustache was trimmed. "I see you got the roses."

Rhea set the bottle down. "Thank you. They're lovely."

He still stood at the door, his hands in his pockets. "They can't compare to what these eyes are takin' in."

Rhea's cheeks grew warm. Flames began to erupt to life inside of her. She felt bashful. Quickly she thought of something to change the subject. "How... how was your trip?"

"Later. I've missed you." Trey came over and gathered her up in his arms. Rhea welcomed his kiss and seemed to float in his embrace. His touch was enough to make her forget everything else.

At the sound of Mona clearing her throat, Rhea pulled away and Trey stood up straight. "If you two will excuse me," said Mona, "I have to run. I'll be late for work." Mona slipped out the door before they could answer. After she was gone, Trey led Rhea over to the couch and they sat down.

"Hey, I've got some news for you. Been doin' a little diggin' while I was away."

Rhea couldn't imagine what he was talking about. He pulled a piece of paper from his shirt pocket. "What is it?"

"It's about your fiancé, Parker Sherwin."

Rhea drew in a quick breath. "Parker?"

"That's right."

Rhea stared at him. News of Parker? What kind of news could Trey mean? "Well, don't keep me in suspense. What did you find out?"

Trey unfolded the paper. "This is a copy of the report from the Forest Service. It gives all the facts about Parker's death. Here, let me read some of it." He sniffed, then began: "Search party in cooperation with the sheriff's department recovered the body at Flatiron Mesa. Witnesses claim Sherwin, acting as crew boss, left his party to go after a member of his crew who panicked ..."

Rhea's head swam. "Stop, Trey! I can't stand it."

"Well, this isn't all," he said. "I've got a copy of his death certificate." He dug into his pants pocket.

"No!" Rhea jumped up. "I don't want to see it!"

"But it's proof, Rhea ... proof that Parker's dead."

"You came over here just to tell me *this*?" Rhea was livid. "First you slip off to Texas and don't bother to tell me where you're going, or *who* you're going to see ... and you don't even bother to let me know when you're coming back."

"I didn't know," Trey protested.

"No, you were obviously too involved with personal business," she blurted.

"I had an obligation." Trey stood up. "Gosh dang, I thought I was finally gettin' through to you, but you're so blinded by your obsession over Parker ... "

"Everything was fine until you brought him up."

"Can you blame me?" Trey cried. "Every time I try to get close to you, he's cuttin' in! You won't let go of him!"

Unable to stand another moment, Rhea ran off to her room and slammed the door. A moment later she heard Trey swear. She heard the front door close behind him. She went to the window to look out and saw Trey get into his truck and drive away.

Damn him, Rhea chided. The evening could have ended so differently. It could have been ... wonderful. She collapsed onto her bed, then caught sight of Parker's smiling face on her headboard. She grabbed the picture in the glass frame.

"Damn you, Parker!" Rhea hurled the frame in frustration across the room. Glass exploded and fragments fell in every direction. Rhea buried her head into her pillow and sobbed.

The next morning Rhea awoke to the rapid song of a ruby-crowned kinglet in the tall spruce outside her window. She lay in bed, reluctant to shed the cocoon of warm covers. She strained to remember the words Parker had used to describe the kinglet's song: "*See, see, see, see. Where? Where? Where? Look at me! Look at me! Look at me!*"

It was time to get up. Even though it was Saturday and there were no classes, she had planned to work over at the Lawrences' condominium. When she finally sat up, she saw the pieces of broken glass from Parker's picture across the room. Guilt swept over her and she touched her bare feet to the cold floor. The mornings were already getting colder and she hadn't closed her window last night.

Rhea retrieved the photograph of Parker, being careful not to step on the glass fragments. Fortunately, the picture was undamaged. She blinked away tears as she looked into Parker's smiling face, then held the picture between her breasts. "Forgive me, darling," she breathed. She sank back onto her pillow and closed her eyes. Memories from last summer surfaced.

Exactly one week before the wedding, Rhea had been going crazy trying to get everything done. She had mailed out the invitations and had personally invited all the people at the Forest Service, as well as her closest friends at the Music School. She wrote up a list of things to do that day. One of the most important items was to go over to Mrs. Daley's and try on her wedding dress. She had found a lady in Aspen who designed and sewed formal gowns. Rhea couldn't wait to try on the dress.

Another thing she had to do was reserve rooms for her parents and Parker's family. They would be flying in sometime on Thursday. How wonderful it would be to see her parents. As for Parker's family, Rhea had been too busy with wedding preparations to worry about meeting them, but she knew she'd like them. If only Parker would get back from the fire so he could help her tie up all these loose ends.

Mona offered to help. She asked Rhea what she could do.

"I wish there was something you could do," said Rhea. "But I just have so much on my mind."

"Well, can I at least go along with you somewhere?"

Rhea let her roommate go with her to Mrs. Daley's. They drove Parker's car. The dress was in need of a hem, but it looked lovely on Rhea when she tried it on. The lace sleeves and scoop neck fit snugly against her slender figure. The skirt was full with a ruffle. Mrs. Daley made several adjustments with the veil and train. Mona sat, oohing and ahhing the whole time. When they left Mrs. Daley's, Mona suggested they stop somewhere for lunch.

"Oh, I don't have time to eat today," said Rhea. "I've got too much to do."

"Of course you're going to eat," insisted Mona. "Do you want to collapse from hunger while walking down that aisle?"

"I ate breakfast."

"Well, I'm famished," said Mona. "I'm going to eat, whether I fit into my maid-of-honor dress or not."

After much protesting, Rhea gave in and Mona directed her to a little patio café at the Airport Business Center. Then, when Rhea saw the girls from the Forest Service, she realized something was up. As she and Mona joined them at a long table, Rhea noticed the pile of brightly colored packages tied with silver and gold ribbons.

"Surprise!" they all yelled.

Rhea blushed. They had gotten together to throw a bridal shower for her. As embarrassed as she was, Rhea felt flattered. While they waited for their lunch to be served, Rhea was coerced into unwrapping her gifts.

"Thank you, everyone," she said afterwards. "I just hope Parker gets back." She learned that more oak brush had caught fire down by Rifle. The blaze had been contained yesterday, Marie explained, but then that morning the wind had shifted and now the fire was again out of control.

"Oh no," groaned Rhea. "I suppose that means Parker will be delayed."

"Not necessarily," said Janet, "though it is hard to tell sometimes."

"I wouldn't worry about him if I were you," said Marie. "After all, Parker's been fighting fires for seven years."

"And it's really not as dangerous as some people like to think," added Janet. "I've been on a couple of small fires myself."

"I'll bet he'll be back tonight," someone else piped in.

"Tomorrow at the latest," assured Janet.

Rhea hoped they were right. The shower ended abruptly because everyone from the Forest Service had to return to work.

"They were so good to throw me a shower," Rhea whispered as her fingers smoothed the rough edges of Parker's photograph. "And they cared about you more than you ever knew."

After Rhea dressed and ate, she rode her bike to the Lawrences' condominium. Work helped to get her mind off Trey and last night's upsetting scene. When she got home later that afternoon, Mona told her Trey had been calling her all day.

"He's really hot for you," said Mona. "It must have been some evening you two had last night."

Rhea sighed. "I'm going jogging. If Trey calls again, tell him I won't be home the rest of the evening."

Mona looked stricken. "What? You don't want to talk to him? Why not? What happened between you two?"

Before Rhea could make up some excuse, the telephone rang. Mona shrugged and went to her room. Rhea was tempted to just let the phone ring, but she felt herself drawn to it. Her hand reached out and picked up the receiver as if by some guiding force. "Hello," she said.

"Rhea? Aw, Rhea, finally! Did you know I've been trying to get you since this morning?" There was an urgency in Trey's voice that melted her. "Are you there?"

"Yes, I'm here," she replied.

"Good. I want to be with you tonight. Want to come over to my place?"

Rhea's heart began to hammer. "All right," she heard herself say.

Trey told her he'd be by to pick her up, then they hung up. Flutters of anticipation filled Rhea as she awaited the arrival of Trey's blue truck. Everything was going to turn out all right, she felt. Her anger had drained. She was being given a second chance. *Tonight*, she promised herself, *I won't let Parker come between us.* For once he was on time and grinned as she walked out to meet him.

"So, you got a new job while I was away," Trey remarked as he drove out of Aspen.

Rhea told him briefly about it. "Unfortunately, it will end after next week." She sighed. "I seem to be doomed to short-term employment. What about you? How much longer will Nickelson Creek Ranch stay open?"

"Through huntin' season," said Trey. "But ol' John replaced me when I said I was takin' off."

"You mean, you don't have a job anymore?"

Trey certainly didn't appear upset about it. He reached out and drew Rhea toward him, keeping his eyes on the road as they drove to the house in Snowmass Village. "Hey, it's okay. This is Aspen, remember?"

Rhea snuggled against Trey's shoulder. When they arrived at the house in Melton Ranch, Trey shut off the motor and kissed her. His leather, masculine smell still provoked an overpowering desire in her and she responded hungrily to his deep kisses.

Finally, Trey suggested they go inside. "I bought some T-bones," he said. "There's a charbroiler on the back deck. You hungry?"

Now that she thought about it, Rhea admitted she was starved. It felt good to be back at the luxurious chalet. She kept having to remind herself that it really belonged to someone else and Trey was merely the house sitter. He expertly prepared the steaks while she watched, admiring him and unable to get over how his haircut had changed him. Then she thought more about it and recalled his purpose for going to Texas. Had he been required to cut his hair for his paying lady friend?

Trey caught her stare. "Somethin' wrong, honeybabe? Why're you starin' at me like that?"

Rhea shook the thought off and came over to help him set two places at the patio table. She had almost wiped the agonizing memory away. She wanted to ask him right out and tell him what Chance had said, but she knew if she did Trey would just get mad. It would ruin the evening.

After the steaks, he lit a fire in the living room fireplace and they sat on cushions as the sky faded to lavender outside the huge windows. The mellow burgundy wine Trey had opened had given Rhea a soft buzz. She struggled to push Parker's memory out of her mind as Trey held her and began to nuzzle her cheek with his chin. She was determined *not* to repeat an episode like last night.

"I've waited so long to hold you again, Rhea. All the time I was gone, I couldn't stop thinking about you."

How she wanted to believe his words. Rhea closed her eyes, relaxed by the tender strokes of his fingers. When he kissed her, she thought, *not even a postcard ...*

Trey withdrew. "What's wrong?"

Rhea sighed. "Nothing."

"No, you're uptight. Wanna talk about it?"

"Really, I'm fine."

He let go of her and they both sat upright and stared into the curling flames that licked the wood. "Well, I know what you're thinking—how it was when *he* made love to you."

Rhea swallowed the last of her wine and set the glass on the hearth. "You're wrong about that," she said. "Parker and I never made love." She drew in a breath for courage and looked right at him. "Parker insisted we wait. I wanted to, but he ..." Her lip trembled and angrily she erased a tear from her eyelid. "Darn it, Trey, I was determined *not* to talk about Parker tonight."

Trey put his arms around her. "No. Go ahead if it makes you feel better."

"Every time we ..." It was difficult for her, but she couldn't stop now. "Whenever Parker and I started to ..."

"What was his excuse?" asked Trey.

"I don't know." She sighed. "He'd always come up with some

damn excuse."

"Well, any guy who'd turn down a fantastic lady like yourself must have been deranged ... or gay."

Rhea pulled away from him. "Parker was *not* gay!"

"I didn't say he was. But considering his problem ..."

Rhea stared at him. "What problem?"

Trey shrugged. "Come on, Rhea, you know what I'm referrin' to."

"No, I don't think I do."

"Rhea, surely he told *you*."

"Told me what?"

"Forget I mentioned it."

"Trey! Tell me what you mean."

Trey picked up the poker and rolled a couple of the logs in the fire. "Well, not every man would be considerate enough to think about his partner before his own needs. I think if I had been in Parker's place ..."

Rhea felt herself getting flushed. "Trey Michaels, if you don't tell me what you're talking about, I'm leaving!"

The fire crackled and a log snapped as Trey looked into her face. "You don't know, do you?"

"That does it." She got to her feet, but Trey grabbed her arm and pulled her down.

"I told you I did a little diggin'," he said. "When I did, I never expected to find out Parker Sherwin had an incurable condition. I would have thought he had told you he was HIV positive."

If the ceiling had caved in on them just then, Rhea could not have been more stricken with horror. She could only stare back at Trey, then into the flames. *Parker ... HIV positive*? It had to be a scandalous lie. It was Trey's attempt at making Parker look bad. Besides, how could Trey—who had never known Parker—have such knowledge?

"Rhea, I'm sorry you had to find out this way. I thought ..."

"No, you're not," she said hotly. "I'm going home. If you can't drive me, I'll ... I'll hitchhike!" She stood up and started out.

Trey scrambled to his feet. "Rhea, wait! Don't go!"

After what she had just heard, Rhea knew she couldn't stay.

She fought off his attempts to restrain her as she started down the lawn in the dark.

"All right, all right ... I'll drive you home."

Rhea climbed into the truck, but sat as close to the window as possible. She refused to look at Trey. Her mind was in a turmoil. It was all she could do to keep from crying. They didn't speak until they got into Aspen and pulled up in front of her apartment. Then Trey apologized again.

"What a vicious thing to say about Parker," snapped Rhea.

"Rhea, I would never make up a thing like that," said Trey. "I can't believe he never told you. What was he going to do—surprise you on your wedding night?"

Rhea tried to slap him, but Trey gripped her wrist before it met his face. "You liar!" she cried.

"Honest, Rhea, I'd never lie to you."

"How dare you?" she challenged. "You couldn't even tell me the truth about your little caper in Texas! You think I don't know about you and your ... your ..."

"I didn't want to upset you," Trey interrupted. "And who told you anything about it anyway?"

Rhea couldn't hold back the tears any longer. Sobs choked her as she struggled to open the stuck door. Trey had to climb out and help her.

"Don't bother to call me," she told him. "I never want to see you again!"

"Aw, Rhea, can't we work this out? If you don't believe I'm tellin' the truth, just ask somebody who knew Parker."

"*I* knew Parker! I knew him and loved him more than anyone else on this earth. And he loved me too much to keep something like that from me!" Rhea ran to her door without looking back.

Fumbling with her key, she let herself in and didn't turn on any lights. A dark void was all she wanted right now, a place to escape ... from everything. Mostly she knew she couldn't look at one of Parker's pictures right now. *What if Trey had been telling the truth?*

13

*R*hea picked up a magazine in the waiting room of Doctor Bernard. She began flipping through the pages when a nurse in a pastel blue uniform approached her.

"Rhea Sinclair?" The nurse smiled at her.

Rhea set the magazine down and stood up.

"Come on back," said the nurse. She led Rhea into the examining room and started to take her blood pressure. "Have you been here before?"

"I'm not sick," Rhea told her. "I just want to talk to Doctor Bernard."

"Well, the doctor should be with you in a few minutes."

"Thank you." Rhea looked around. Her nerves were on edge and she was scared. Was she wasting her time being here? What if the answer the doctor gave her was not the one she wanted to hear?

Several minutes elapsed before a light rap on the door broke the silence. Then Doctor Bernard entered the room. He was a kindly, older man with glasses and short gray hair. He wore a casual brown shirt and a stethoscope hung from his neck.

"Hello, Miss Sinclair," he said. "Why don't we go across the hall into my office?"

Rhea followed him. He closed the door and beckoned her into a chair, then took a seat behind his desk.

"Now what can I do for you? My nurse mentioned that you wanted to talk to me."

"That's right."

"She mentioned that your fiancé was a patient of mine."

"Yes, he was," said Rhea. "Parker Sherwin."

The doctor seemed to sense her reluctance. "I take it your visit has something to do with the two of you."

"Yes." Rhea swallowed. "Parker died, you know."

"Yes, I know," the doctor said softly. He pushed a button on his intercom and then spoke into it. "Sharon, will you please bring me the file on Parker Sherwin?" Then he turned back to Rhea. "How can I be of help?"

Rhea drew in a slow breath. "I need to know…was Parker in poor health?"

Doctor Bernard smiled. "Actually, Parker was quite fit. If I remember correctly, he was a runner."

"That's right," said Rhea.

"Did you have a particular concern?"

"Well, I was wondering why he saw you. I mean, he did see you last summer. Once was for the physical, so we could get our marriage license."

The nurse entered the room with a file folder, which she handed to Doctor Bernard. Then she left.

"We'll just have a look here." The doctor opened the file. "Usually I don't discuss records without the patient's permission. But in your case—seeing as how you were Parker's fiancée… hmm." He adjusted his glasses as he flipped a page.

"Please, doctor, I have to know. Did Parker have HIV?" Rhea's lip trembled.

Doctor Bernard closed the file and regarded her sternly. "Yes, Miss Sinclair. Parker did have HIV. But surely you knew about this already."

Tears spilled from Rhea's eyes and she turned away. *Oh God, no … Trey was right!*

"I'm afraid HIV is a growing affliction in our population," said Doctor Bernard. "There is no cure. Perhaps you'd like me to test you. As unpleasant as it may be, people do manage to live normal lives."

"I don't need a test." Tears continued to spill down Rhea's face.

"Are you sure?"

Rhea stood up to leave. "Thank you, doctor." A sob broke loose.

"Wait a minute, before you go ..." The doctor stood up. "Maybe we need to discuss this." He put a restraining hand on her shoulder. "Please sit down."

Rhea did as he said and tried to calm herself. She learned Parker had contracted the virus many years ago, probably from his first wife. A lot of things were making sense to Rhea now. He had apparently not wanted to infect her. "But why didn't he *tell* me?" she cried.

Doctor Bernard sighed. "I'm afraid we'll never know the answer to that."

"Oh, I intend to get an answer," Rhea blurted out. "He's got a lot of explaining to do."

"Excuse me?"

Rhea's shock turned to anger. "He's had plenty of opportunities to tell me." Suddenly she realized the impact of her words.

"Rhea, tell me something," prompted the doctor. "Do you... communicate with Parker?"

Rhea realized she had been running at the mouth and had said too much. What did the doctor think? If she admitted that yes, she actually held conversations with Parker on the jogging trail, he would certainly think she was insane.

The doctor picked up a pen and began to scribble something on a notepad. "I know someone who might be able to help you."

"A psychiatrist, you mean?" Rhea dabbed at her eyes.

Doctor Bernard kept a straight face. "Do *you* think you need a psychiatrist?"

"Forget what I said. I'm just so upset."

He tore off the paper and handed it to her. "Here."

"What is it, a prescription?"

"No, I am not referring you to a psychiatrist," said the doctor. "This is the address of a personal friend. She goes by the name of Sister Laurus. She lives right here in Aspen. She's had a lot of experience with this kind of thing and I believe you should give her a call."

"A medium?"

Doctor Bernard nodded and smiled as Rhea left his office. Rhea didn't know what to think about an M.D. who referred his patients to a psychic. But then, she had to remind herself this was Aspen and a wide variety of philosophies flourished in town. She had never seriously considered consulting a medium before, but she knew it was a fact that Parker's spirit jogged with her. Their conversations were real and intelligent, even if they were more on a level beyond most people's understanding.

Rhea stuffed the slip of paper into her backpack and walked out of the doctor's office, numb from what she had discovered.

The week passed quickly. Rhea did not hear anything from Trey. She thought about calling him to beg his forgiveness. She knew her words had been unjustified. She had called Trey a liar when he had been telling the truth about Parker's affliction. How he had found out was a riddle. Apparently someone had known about it—perhaps Bill Marshall, the district ranger. But it didn't matter anymore.

She still could not forget about Trey's long absence. He hadn't even had the decency to tell her his reason for going to Texas. The longer time went by and he didn't call, the deeper she ached. And—try as she did—she couldn't wipe Trey Michaels out of her mind.

The job with Arthur Lawrence ended when Rhea handed over the last of his musical compositions. He, Elizabeth and Betsy would soon leave Aspen for their home back East. They thought the Music Festival had been highly successful and looked forward to next year.

"Will you be back in Aspen next summer, Rhea?" Elizabeth asked as she wrote out Rhea's last paycheck.

"I don't know, Mrs. Lawrence." Rhea couldn't bear to think of her future. She began to dread the emptiness that lay ahead in her life. She was tired of scrounging for a living and her heart ached worse than before.

When she was strolling across campus after her last meeting with Caroline Bent, Jerome intercepted her. "Rhea, wait up," he called.

"Oh hi, Jerome."

"You sound down," he remarked.

"Do I?"

"Well, I just wanted to confirm our plans for tomorrow night," said Jerome. "It's the last Tent concert, you know. I wouldn't want to miss it."

Rhea agreed to go and said she'd meet him at the usual time.

"No." Jerome placed a plump white hand on her arm. "Tomorrow I'll come by and get you."

Rhea stared after him, puzzled by his action. Why did Jerome appear strange all of a sudden?

Mona was crushed to hear of Rhea's decision to move out. "No!" she cried. "You can't mean it. Why do you want to leave Aspen? You know you love it here."

"Really, Mona, what choice do I have?" Rhea shook her head. "I've already phoned my parents. They're sending me the money to fly home."

"Oh Rhea, you just can't! What about Trey? Have you told him?"

"We're through."

"So that's what this is all about."

Rhea sighed. "No, Mona. It's been building up for weeks now—my money situation, that is."

"And the answer is to fly home to Mom and Pop, right?"

"There's no reason to be sarcastic about it," snapped Rhea.

"I think you should at least call Trey and tell him," said Mona. "He might have something to say about your leaving."

"No way. And don't go opening your mouth to Chance either. I don't want Trey to know."

"You say that, but you can't mean it."

Not wanting to argue further, Rhea went to her room and began packing. In her closet she came across a box containing shower gifts from the women at the Forest Service last summer. All wedding gifts had been returned, but she had held onto the shower gifts when the girls insisted they did not want them back.

Sitting back on her bed, Rhea's memory returned to that day almost a year ago. She recalled how she had gone to bed that night, too tired to worry about Parker still being away. She dreamed about her wedding day. In her dream only a handful of guests sat waiting in the church. They had been sitting for hours—waiting. Then Bill Marshall, the Aspen District Ranger— who was going to be Parker's best man—arrived in his govern- ment uniform instead of a tuxedo. Worse yet, Mona sat stuffing her face with tortilla chips. Rhea kept worrying about the crumbs being left on the chapel carpet.

Her dream ended in the middle of the sound of the doorbell ringing. As Rhea awoke, she realized the doorbell must have rung at least three or four times. The first light of morning streamed through her bedroom window as she threw the covers aside and got up.

Thinking it might be Parker, Rhea pulled on her robe and hurried to open the door. To her surprise, there stood Bill Marshall, the district ranger, wearing his sheepskin coat. He held his ranger hat in his hands.

"Bill!" Rhea stepped aside to let him in. "What brings you here so early in the morning?" She stared at his solemn face. The district ranger was just forty, with dark eyes and curly hair. He looked as though he hadn't slept in a week. Aware of the chill from outside, Rhea invited him in.

"I'm sorry to intrude on you at this ungodly hour, Rhea."

"What's wrong, Bill? Is Parker back in Aspen yet?"

Bill stood still and didn't answer right away. Rhea started to feel a terrible cold that had nothing to do with the fall weather. Bill motioned her over to a chair and she sat down. "God, how I hate to be the one ..." he started to say. There was a quaver in his voice.

"Bill, what is it?" Rhea began to shake. "Where is Parker? Is he all right?"

The district ranger's voice trembled and his words were smothered with emotion. "I'm afraid it's rather bad news, Rhea. Parker's dead."

The cold was unbearable just then. Rhea could only stare at Bill as he fought to keep from falling apart. The man had obviously been through an ordeal.

The first wave of disbelief and shock swept over Rhea. "No," she said, "it can't be. Tell me he's just outside … waiting to surprise me."

"Rhea, I'm sorry." Bill fought with his emotions a moment or two before he began to explain. "We don't know exactly what happened. One of the guys he was with at Flatiron Mesa got scared and started to run. Parker was crew boss and must have felt responsible. He went after him and that's the last anyone saw of him. We think he might have fallen and been knocked unconscious. He wasn't able to move out of the burn area."

The rest became a blur to Rhea. Disbelief soon dissolved into horror as she saw her future and all her plans topple. Her life was ruined. The man she loved and was going to marry in six days was no more. There would be no wedding. There would be no more of those warm fireside nights at the log house. Never again would she be able to look into Parker's loving blue eyes, or hear his soft, gentle voice calling to her.

Bill Marshall stayed with Rhea that morning until Mona came home. It was the beginning of Rhea's worst nightmare.

The next morning Rhea had an appointment with Sister Laurus. At first she had trouble believing the woman was a psychic medium. Sister Laurus was a housewife living in the west end of town. She had three children and a house full of cats. Her place appeared untidy and dark, but Sister Laurus herself didn't seem out of the ordinary. She wore jeans, a summer top and a scarf on her head. She shooed her children out to play, then invited Rhea into one of the bedrooms.

"Just make yourself comfortable," said Sister Laurus. "I'll throw some clothes in the dryer and be right with you."

Rhea sat in a chair in the small bedroom where the curtains had been drawn. She noticed a computer on the desk and a bed that was sloppily made. Rhea wondered if Sister Laurus would start moaning and fall into a trance. *Oh, why did I come here?* she fretted.

"Stay outside!" she heard the medium yell at her kids. "Have Angela take you to the park." Then she came back into the bedroom and closed the door. "Okay, let's get started," she said.

Rhea sat straight in her chair and braced herself for the worst. Sister Laurus took a seat a few feet from Rhea and closed her eyes, bending slightly forward as she rested her forehead in her hands.

"Start by giving me your full name," said the medium.

Rhea gave the information Sister Laurus requested, and after a long pause the woman began to speak in a normal voice. Her eyes remained closed as she drew in a few deep breaths.

"Your mother and father are living?"

"Yes," Rhea replied.

There was another long pause. The tumble of the dryer from outside the room filled the void as another minute passed. Sister Laurus did not move. Then she said, "Your brother says you should write to your parents more often. They worry about you, he says."

"I don't have any brothers or sisters," said Rhea.

Sister Laurus opened her eyes. "Yes, you do. There's a definite feeling here of a brother. I can't deny it. He's in spirit now."

A brother? No way, thought Rhea. *Sister Laurus must be a fake.* But she kept her doubts to herself as the medium continued. She began rattling off things that had to do with Rhea's parents. She described her father's and mother's relationship and mentioned a couple of health problems they might watch for. Rhea was impressed at how closely Sister Laurus came to accurately describing her parents' personalities. Could she have known them somehow? It didn't seem likely.

"Music is important to you," Sister Laurus said. "I get the feeling it could become even more important to you now. You should not get discouraged with it." She opened her eyes and looked at Rhea. "Were you thinking about giving it up?"

"What do you mean?" asked Rhea.

"Your enthusiasm seems to be tapering off." Sister Laurus closed her eyes. "There is a spirit here who keeps trying to break in. He says you must not give up your music."

Rhea sat on the edge of her seat. "Who is he?"

Sister Laurus shook her head, her eyes still closed. "I can't seem to ... he wants to take over. Ask me a question. Maybe that will help."

Rhea paused, then asked, "Is Parker there?"

"Parker ... Parker ... what's his full name?"

Rhea told her and immediately the medium responded.

"Wait! Yes, he is. He is with you constantly, he says." She kept her eyes closed as she continued. "I am quite sure he is the one who cut in." Then she said, "He died tragically."

"Yes." Rhea began to grow excited.

"I get the feeling of heat ... extreme heat ... and not being able to breathe," said Sister Laurus.

Rhea wondered if the medium remembered reading about Parker's death and the fact that he had died in a forest fire. Perhaps she was speculating all of this for Rhea's benefit. Still, it was an intriguing show.

Sister Laurus sighed. "I believe he had a hard time when he died. He feels very close to you."

"We were to be married," said Rhea.

"I can see that now. But I think there might have been problems ahead if you two had gotten together in this life."

"What kind of problems?"

"I mean one of you might have been dissatisfied," said the medium. "I don't mean you were not suited to one another. You were. That's plain. It's possible Parker is your soulmate." She paused, then said, "But there is something there ... one of you would have been bitter and upset about something."

"What about jogging?" asked Rhea.

The question puzzled Sister Laurus. "Jogging?" Then she laughed. "Oh yes, Parker says he wanted to keep you at it. He says not to quit now."

"But does he really jog with me?" asked Rhea. "Is it Parker at my side, or is it just my imagination?"

Sister Laurus shook her head, trying hard to concentrate. "He's blocking me again. Go on to something else."

Rhea thought of another question. "What can you tell me about Trey Michaels?"

"Trey Michaels ... Trey Michaels ..." The medium pondered for half a minute. Suddenly a grin broke out on her face. "Oh yes! Trey!" Then suddenly her face went dark.

"What is it?" asked Rhea.

"I don't know. I can't ... honestly, I don't know what's happening here. I've never had a reading before where one spirit dominates. It's like... the answer is being blocked." Finally she opened her eyes and sighed. "I'm sorry. I can't get through. Do you have any more questions?"

Rhea wanted to ask a lot more questions, but what was the use? "Just one," she said. "Am I doing the right thing moving away from Aspen?"

Sister Laurus closed her eyes again. "Hmm ... I don't really see anything positive coming from it. By moving away from Aspen, you will not be leaving any of your problems behind. On the other hand, if you stay ..."

"If I stay, what?" prompted Rhea.

"It's ... it's unclear." Sister Laurus opened her eyes. "I'm sorry. My mind seems to be a blank all of a sudden."

After Rhea paid the fee, she rode her bike home and pondered all that Sister Laurus had said. It was amazing what Sister Laurus had picked up on her parents, and even the stuff about Parker couldn't have been made up on the spot. So why couldn't Sister Laurus tell her anything about Trey? Or her future? Had she been keeping back something dreadful that she thought Rhea couldn't bear to hear? Or had Parker intentionally blocked the information?

When Jerome came by that evening to pick her up for the concert, Rhea tried to act cheerful, but she could not hide her growing depression. After the concert they stopped in a bar to discuss the end of the Music Festival. Rhea finally told Jerome she was leaving Aspen.

In the dim light Jerome's mouth fell open. It was the first time Rhea had seen her friend anything other than calm and undisturbed. He fixed his gaze upon her face. "You are leaving?" he asked incredulously.

Rhea lifted her drink to her lips and sipped. "Why not?" she murmured. "You're leaving too, aren't you?"

"Well ... no," he said. "I wasn't going to tell you till tonight because I wanted to surprise you."

Rhea stared at him curiously. Was Jerome Hodges blushing, or was it merely the lighting? "You mean you've decided to stay in Aspen?"

He adjusted his glasses. "I was hoping ..." He cleared his throat. "Actually, Rhea, our friendship has come to mean an awful lot to me this summer."

Rhea smiled at him warmly. "What a nice thing to say, Jerome." She took another sip. "You're a terrific friend too. I'll write to you. You can count on that."

"I wish you weren't moving," said Jerome. His heavy face seemed to sink into a blob.

Rhea stared into her half-empty glass. "It's really been a wonderful summer, hasn't it? Especially the trip to Snowmass Lake. I'm glad you talked me into going along."

Jerome sighed morosely. "Yes, that was certainly the highlight of my summer, too—even though I did have that close call."

Longings poured into Rhea's soul at the memory of Snowmass Lake. Visions of herself and Trey and the beauty of the aspens and the greenness of the lake all took hold of her and she paid no attention to Jerome's ramblings. She remembered Trey watching her as they had made their climb on the horses. Trey had kissed her on the shore. She would never forget the night they had spent together in her sleeping bag, the warmth of his strong body close to hers. How she missed the leather and hay scent that had aroused her along with his tender kisses. And now she would never feel that wonderful again. Not even Parker had come close to making her feel so much a woman.

"And I really hoped we could make plans to see more of each other," Jerome was saying. "Rhea?" He snapped his fingers in front of her face. "You okay?"

Rhea's reverie ended and she tipped her glass and drank another swallow. Her head began to fog from the rum. "I'm sorry, Jerome. What were you saying?"

"Weren't you listening?" The tone of his voice surprised her. Could this be the level-headed, ever tolerant Jerome she had known for more than a year?

She didn't answer, but finished her drink.

"Hey, you made quick work of those daiquiris," said Jerome. "I'd better take you home."

Rhea did not protest. She felt dizzy and suspended from everything around her as Jerome stood up. She heard the clatter of money being dropped onto the table, and then Jerome led her out. When they got to her apartment, Rhea was embarrassed to discover she had dozed off in the car. Jerome offered to help her to the door.

"Oh, I can walk," Rhea protested, but Jerome insisted on helping her anyway. She couldn't wait to fall into bed. She stumbled as they reached the porch steps. "Now look who's the clumsy one," Rhea giggled.

"Are you sure you're all right?"

"I'm fine," said Rhea. Suddenly her throat quivered and she began to cry.

"What's the matter?" asked Jerome.

"I don't really want to leave Aspen." Rhea sobbed and fell against Jerome. It felt good to let it all out. He was like a huge cushion holding her. She hoped she wasn't getting his shoulder wet.

"Then don't," Jerome replied softly, a fat hand stroking her hair. "Please don't leave Aspen. I don't want to lose you."

Rhea stopped crying and gently pulled away, still sniffling. He was serious. He was holding her and it meant something entirely different to Jerome than it did to her. She hadn't meant to lead him on. Not at all!

Jerome looked at her. "Would you like me to kiss you?"

Rhea looked around. *How was she going to get out of this one?* she wondered. She couldn't hurt Jerome's feelings. He was her kindest, dearest friend. Yet, she couldn't bear the thought of having to kiss the big ox. If she told him no, would he be crushed? Rhea smiled awkwardly. "I think I'll just go in now." She put her hand on the doorknob.

Clearing his throat, Jerome stepped back. "Well, then ..." He thrust out his right hand. "Good night, Rhea."

Rhea reluctantly shook his hand. *Such a strange man.* "Good night, Jerome." She was starting to sober up as she watched him walk away. He almost tripped in the street and she smiled. Had he gotten the message? That had certainly been a close one.

As Rhea let herself into her apartment, she made up her mind that—like it or not—she now had no choice but to leave Aspen.

14

*T*wo days before her scheduled flight out of Aspen, Rhea had everything packed except some clothes and immediate needs she could gather up at the last minute. Since the Music Festival had ended, she had become withdrawn. Amid Jerome's persistent pleas to go out with him, she preferred to stay home, close to the piano she would not play again. One piano was like another, it was true. But this piano—in this apartment—had been hers during the happiest—and saddest—days of her life.

Her parents looked forward to her homecoming and were glad she had "finally come to her senses," as her mother had put it.

Rhea had packed all the pictures of Parker in a box except for one. She had bought a new glass frame for the picture she had smashed the night of her temper tantrum. Parker's face smiled at her now, cheerful and alive. Yet he hadn't been on the jogging trail since before her reading with Sister Laurus.

Rhea went over in her mind the things the medium had told her. One thing that had come to light was the fact that she had indeed once had a brother. On the telephone Rhea had jokingly told her mother about Sister Laurus' comments. That's when Rhea learned that her mother had lost a child before she had become pregnant with Rhea.

"Mom, how come you never told me?"

"Because it hurt too much, I suppose," said her mother. "It was a heartbreaking thing that happened and I couldn't talk about it."

Rhea had not told her parents the real reason why she had seen the psychic. In her private thoughts she pondered the things

Sister Laurus had said about Parker. She sensed that he was more at peace because she had seen the medium. But her own depression had only deepened.

As she sat at the piano her fingers began to experiment with chords and soon Rhea fell into a George Harrison tune. Mona entered the room and leaned against the piano. Rhea finished the song and looked up at her roommate.

"How are you doing?" asked Mona.

"Okay."

"I certainly am going to miss the music in this apartment," said Mona.

Rhea stood up. "Mona, please, don't start in on me again. Maybe I *am* making the biggest mistake of my life—as you seem to think I am—but I'm still leaving on Wednesday and that's final."

"I'm not here to harass you," said Mona. "How would you like to go rafting tomorrow?"

"Rafting? You've got to be kidding."

"A bunch of us from Gustav's are going. Why don't you join us?"

"No thanks, Mona. I've never been rafting before."

"So? Neither have I." Mona made a face. "I can't even swim!"

Rhea smiled. "Thanks for asking, but I don't think so."

"Well, have you got anything better to do on your last day in Aspen?" asked Mona.

Rhea remembered that Jerome had begged her to spend some time with him tomorrow. He had been calling frequently, and during their last telephone conversation she had gotten the distinct impression that he was lovesick over her. She had managed to avoid him all week but was running out of excuses. If she went away on a rafting trip with Mona's friends, that would mean she would be too tired out at the end of the day to spend much time with her musician friend.

"Rhea, come on. You need to get out of this apartment," said Mona. "What do you say?"

"Well, how many people are going?"

Mona counted on her fingers. "There's me and Chance …

Gina, Susie, Don … there's eight of us."

"Chance is going?" Rhea made a face.

"It's going to be blast! And Don's experienced. He says the river's not too dangerous right now. It should be a lot of fun."

"Oh Mona, you know what a chicken I am." The phone rang right then. Afraid that it was Jerome calling her again, Rhea quickly made up her mind. "Okay, Mona, I'll go."

Mona cheered, then ran to answer the phone. "I promise you won't be sorry!"

The next morning two of Mona's friends from the restaurant came by. Rhea climbed into the back seat of the car with Mona and they were soon headed forty miles downvalley to Glenwood Springs, where the Roaring Fork River met the Colorado.

"The others will meet us there," Mona explained.

"By the others she means the *men*," said Gina, a wacky redhead who giggled a lot.

Susie was more down to earth. Her long brown hair blew from the open window as she drove. "I hope Mona told you to wear a bathing suit."

"I did." Rhea had her suit on under her clothes. She carried a daypack with suntan lotion, a sweatshirt and some cheese and crackers for lunch.

They parked at a specified lot next to the river in Glenwood Springs. No one else had arrived yet, so they waited a few minutes until Chance's beat-up Jeep pulled alongside of them, followed by a truck towing the rubber raft.

"Everybody out," directed Susie.

The sun was bright and Rhea marveled at the blueness of the Colorado sky as she stretched and inhaled a deep breath of fresh air. The river appeared calm. Maybe this wasn't going to be so treacherous after all.

Car doors slammed as the men got out. Chance approached and Rhea turned and suddenly saw Trey standing next to the truck. She could only stare, wondering what *he* was doing here. Trey regarded her coolly. He didn't smile. Rhea turned her back as Mona and Chance chatted freely.

"Come on, pick up your life jackets over here," called out one of the other men.

"Rhea, come on," coaxed Mona.

"I wish you had told me," Rhea grumbled so no one could hear.

Mona merely grinned at her, then over at Trey, who was helping to get the raft into the river. "Oh, come on, Rhea. Let's just have a good time."

Resentment swelled within Rhea as she reluctantly followed the others to the riverbank. She was still trying to figure out how to strap on the orange life jacket when Trey edged close to her and murmured a "hello" in his familiar deep voice.

"Hi, Trey," she replied without enthusiasm. Glancing up, she saw that he was no longer looking at her, and since he didn't say anything more, she pretended to be busy with her strap.

"Hey, want some help with that?" a masculine voice asked.

Rhea looked up as Don, the one who seemed to be taking charge, reached toward her to fasten the life jacket. He was tall and blond with a beard and mustache. His skin was burned red from the sun. Rhea was aware of Trey watching out the corner of his eye.

"There. Perfect." Don's eyes probed hers. "You're Mona's roommate, aren't you?" He thrust out his hand and she shook it. "I'm Don."

"Do you work at Gustav's?" Rhea asked. He was pumping her hand longer than necessary.

"I'm the bartender." He grinned.

And what a charmer you are, thought Rhea, withdrawing her hand at last. She wondered what Trey thought.

"Let's go, Don!" somebody called.

They all climbed into the raft. Rhea did not sit next to Trey. He sat on the opposite side—between Mona and Gina—not paying any attention to her. Rhea didn't quite know what to do, but when someone handed her a paddle, she followed the example of the others and paddled as instructed.

Don sat beside Rhea and told everyone what to do. The raft floated along slowly at first, bobbing gently with the current as they headed downriver. Rhea was still pouting about how Mona had conned her into this trip. Trey acted as though he didn't want anything to do with her.

"Ooh, this is *so* exciting," squealed Gina.

"Toots, you haven't seen anything yet," scoffed Susie. "Wait'll we hit some rapids."

It wasn't long before the ride became rougher. The bumps were fun, Rhea discovered, as she couldn't help but join in the laughter of the others. Before long she was caught up in the thrills and had almost forgotten the grudge she and Trey were carrying.

At one point they stopped to retrieve a lost paddle. Everyone piled out of the raft and waded to shore to stretch while Don and Chance went after the paddle. Trey sidled up to Rhea.

"Chance didn't tell me you were coming on this trip." He kicked at some stones near the water's edge.

"No, Mona didn't tell me you'd be here either. I think we were set up."

"You're still mad at me, aren't you?" asked Trey.

Rhea looked into his face and started to protest, but he didn't wait for her answer.

"I just found out this is your last day in Colorado. Why are you leaving?"

Rhea sighed. "Does it matter?"

"You're leaving for good, aren't you?" There was such sadness in Trey's eyes, Rhea could hardly bare it.

She nodded. "I have no reason to stay."

Trey was silent. The paddle had been retrieved and everyone piled back into the raft. As Rhea returned to her corner of the raft—paddle in place—she stared into the brown water, its turmoil matching the storm she felt inside. *No reason to stay,* she had said, her heart heavy. He hadn't even asked her what she meant. It was obvious he no longer cared. Her mind drifted back to last fall.

"There's no reason to stay in Aspen. Of course you're coming home with us," Rhea's mother had said to her that dark evening before Parker's funeral. Her parents had flown out to be with her as soon as they could after her telephone call.

Rhea sat in the mortuary chambers, numb from fatigue, her eyes swollen from crying. The mourners had come and gone. The visitation was over, but she remained with her parents and the Sherwins. Rhea lifted her face and could see Parker's parents in their own little corner beside the coffin. His tall blond brother, Fred, had been the most friendly toward her so far. Mr. and Mrs. Sherwin had been tolerantly civil, their shock still blinding them to any outsider's grief over the death of their son.

After having looked forward so long to meeting Parker's parents, Rhea had been disappointed at their coldness. Of course, she knew it had been a terrible blow to them, but she had not expected to be regarded as a total stranger in their eyes.

"Tomorrow your father and I will help you pack," resumed her mother in a low voice. "Believe me, the change will do you a world of good."

"I can't, Mama." Rhea's voice was thick and hoarse from crying. "I'm not going home."

"Why not?" Her mother looked helplessly at her husband, who sat with his hands folded beside them. Her father looked so serious and forlorn in his black suit and tie. "Jim, talk to her."

"No, Mama ... I can't leave Parker," protested Rhea.

Her father put a warm palm upon her arm and smiled. "Rhea, you know already that the Sherwins are flying Parker's body back to California for burial."

A sob escaped as Rhea blew her nose into a soggy handkerchief. She stared across the dim room at the closed casket. "They may have his body," she whimpered, "but his soul is here in Aspen ... with me."

"You'll change your mind in a few days," said her mother.

Before they left the funeral parlor, Rhea approached the coffin one last time. The finely carved mahogany box contained her shattered dreams. How she longed to open the lid and look upon Parker's tall, slender form one last time. She wanted to gaze upon the sleeping face and kiss Parker's lips before he was taken away from her forever. But she knew the fire had caused damage and he was beyond recognition.

Rhea felt the approach of another human being from behind. She spotted the hem of a black dress and high heels, and slowly glanced up at the tall, gray-haired lady standing next to her. Mrs. Sherwin smiled at Rhea for the first time and took hold of her wrist.

"Rhea, dear, what you must be going through," said Mrs. Sherwin. "I'm afraid Mr. Sherwin and myself have been too wrapped up in our own grief to think about your feelings."

"Thank you," Rhea mumbled.

"We loved him very much," continued Parker's mother. "I admit, I regret the fact that you'll never be our daughter-in-law. Tell me. What are your plans now?"

The woman's question seemed out of place somehow. "I really don't know. I haven't thought about it," replied Rhea.

"I suppose you will continue with your musical career. Parker wrote to us about it, you know."

Rhea sniffed. "Marrying Parker was all I wanted." Rhea's voice faltered as a gush of emotion pushed its way up inside her chest.

Fred came up to them then and whispered something to his mother. Mrs. Sherwin moved away and Fred comforted Rhea. He told her all the things she needed to hear then—how much she had meant to his brother, how lucky he had been to have found a woman he wanted to spend the rest of his life with after that bitter first marriage. Fred was like Parker, Rhea discovered. At least partly. He resembled his brother enough to bring solace to Rhea's bereavement. Fred's gentle, consoling manner somehow eased the pain that helped Rhea get through the funeral ceremony the next morning.

The Sherwins left Aspen afterwards. Mrs. Sherwin had already ransacked Parker's log house, gathering all his belongings. Without even asking Rhea first, she had turned Lynx over to the Pitkin County Animal Shelter. Whatever became of the cat, Rhea never found out. It was only due to Fred's kindness that she had been left the four photographs of Parker.

Now, staring into the rushing river water below, Rhea realized her parents would be glad to have her back home again, at least until she could scratch out some plans for her bleak future. Why did it all seem more hopeless now than it had back then?

Somebody passed Rhea a can of beer and she awoke to the present. Rhea opened it and took some long swallows. The sun was high in the sky and the cold, bubbly liquid felt soothing to her throat.

"Rapids ahead," announced Don.

"Oh no! Look out!" squealed Gina.

"Everybody hang onto your beer," somebody called out.

"Forget the beer. Paddle! Don't let the raft tilt too much."

It was a wild run over the rapids, with all of them screaming and laughing, holding on for dear life. Mona was tossed into the center of the raft and had trouble getting back to her place. She was laughing so hard, she kept losing her balance. Tears ran down Rhea's face from laughter as she watched Trey and Chance finally pull her roommate up again. The raft floated down less turbulent waters and everyone had to open a new can of beer.

A couple of hours later, they stopped and had lunch near some gravel pits. The interstate highway with its constant whir of traffic followed the course of the river, but it was far enough away that Rhea could concentrate on the reverence of nature and the changing topography. They had floated through canyons and sandstone cracks, but now the land opened up and the mountains were out of their sight.

Rhea decided to save her cheese and crackers. Greg, who was the chef at Gustav's, had brought along munchies to go with the beer. On a grassy spot beneath some shady cottonwoods, they sat and ate chicken salad sandwiches and deviled eggs wrapped individually in aluminum foil.

"Having a good time?" Don surprised Rhea by placing his hand over hers as they sat next to one another on the shore.

She looked at him and reached for another deviled egg. She wanted to pull her hand away, but didn't want to appear rude.

"Maybe we should do this more often," Don continued.

Rhea stared at their hands.

"Rafting, I mean." Don laughed.

"Oh, I'm afraid not," said Rhea. "You see …"

"The lady's not going to be around after today," Trey interrupted just then. He had gone over to get another beer and now stood over them.

"Oh, that's a shame," said Don. "Here I was hoping to get to know you better." Don seemed to catch the warning look in Trey's eye just then. He let go of Rhea's hand and moved aside. "Have a nice trip—wherever you're going."

Trey sat down next to Rhea and popped the lid off his beer can. For a long moment neither of them spoke. Rhea ate her deviled egg, relieved not to have Don playing up to her anymore. "Want another beer?" Trey asked her.

"No," she replied. "Thanks, though."

He glanced at her and smiled—*finally*. "Don't mention it," he said.

Rhea smiled back at him. She longed for things to be all right between them. She was willing to forgive and forget if only he would let her.

"Are you sorry you came?" Trey asked.

Rhea shook her head. "Not anymore." She noticed Mona and Chance standing next to the water's edge, looking in their direction. She could just hear Mona saying to Chance, "See? It worked."

Trey touched her arm. "You better watch out or you'll turn as red as Don."

Rhea remembered the suntan lotion and burrowed into her daypack for it. She wanted to ask what he had been doing since the last time she had seen him. Had he found work? His situation, she realized, wasn't as pressing as hers. He, at least, had a place to stay—rent-free. But before she could ask any questions, it was time to pack up the lunch leftovers and put the life jackets back on.

This time Trey sat next to Rhea on the raft. The river wound through a more populated area and somebody said they were at Rifle. Rhea rubbed more suntan lotion on herself. She was glad when they were past Rifle. She was reminded of the fact that Parker had died near there. They were soon flying over rough waters once again, struggling to keep the raft at its proper angle.

"Watch out!" cried out Chance. "There's big ones ahead!"

"Oh, no, a suckhole!" somebody shouted.

"Steer! Steer!" screamed Susie, her paddle pitching right and left.

A gush of water sprayed over Rhea and Trey as their end of the raft lifted high, then plunged downward. Rhea gripped the side of the raft as water matted her hair to her head and back. She blinked, worried for a moment that she might be tossed out.

"No! More to the left!" yelled Don.

Amid the screams came wild laughter as the raft twisted and bounced over the rapids. Water flew up and Rhea panicked. This was by far the most dangerous rapids they had gone over. She reached out for Trey to steady herself and felt her body rise.

Suddenly, Rhea felt herself flying through the air. She screamed and the next thing she knew, she hit a wall of cold water and sank beneath the silence of the Colorado River.

15

The shock of the cold and no air to breathe launched Rhea into panic. She surfaced and gasped for breath, struggling to keep her face out of the river. For a long moment she felt helpless and the blazing sun burned her eyes. Water poured into her mouth and she coughed and spluttered, arms flailing. The life jacket forced her to float, but she felt out of control.

Stay calm, for God's sake, she told herself. With all the rocks around her, she hadn't hit any, which seemed a miracle in itself. She remembered she should face downriver. The bright sun continued to blind her as she treaded water and felt the current carrying her.

"Rhea!" voices called. The raft pitched a short ways ahead and all heads were turned in her direction. Then Rhea saw someone else tumble out and people screamed.

Rhea grabbed onto a large log protruding out of the water as the current pulled her past it. She could still feel the force of the water on her waist and legs. The raft disappeared over another rapids among shouts and cries. A moment later, Rhea heard Trey call her name. Glancing over, she saw his head as he swam toward her. It was difficult for him because he had to fight the current.

She waved with one hand as the other clung to the log. "Trey!" she shouted over the roar of rushing water.

"Hold on!" he called, struggling to reach her. He didn't seem to be getting anywhere. She was afraid that if Trey stopped swimming, he would be swept over the rapids just as the raft and its occupants had just done.

Shading her eyes, Rhea noticed the raft again. It appeared in her view as it floated farther away. The six people on board paddled wildly to steady it. She knew sooner or later they'd have it under control and would stop and come back for them.

"Trey, can you make it?" Rhea cried out.

He had made a little progress and was within five yards of her. Rhea's teeth began chattering uncontrollably. The icy river water was starting to affect her. When Trey finally reached her, she was numb and could hardly move. "Come on, let's get to shore," he told her. He placed an arm around her shoulders. "Think you can make it?"

"Yes." Rhea had to let Trey do most the work as they fought to swim their way to the nearest shore. He still held her as they waded in and then dropped onto the sunny river bank. Trey was exhausted and lay back to catch his breath. When Rhea looked up, she saw that the others had managed to get the raft to shore. Don and Greg ran along the rocks toward them.

"Anybody hurt?"

"No, we're okay," Trey called back. He didn't bother to get up.

Rhea was too tired to move. She lay in the grass, shading her eyes from the bright sun. The warm heat soothed her wet skin and it felt good just to lie there.

"Well, we'd better get rolling if we're going to reach the van," prompted Don.

"Do we have to?" Rhea murmured.

"Let's *go*." Don sounded impatient.

Trey grunted, then sat up. "I think the lady needs more time to rest," he said.

"She can rest in the raft," said Don in a hard voice.

Rhea uncovered her eyes to watch Trey and the taller man face each other. A tenseness filled her just then and she sat up straight.

"I don't think I like the way you're orderin' us around," said Trey.

"Come on, you two, knock it off," said Greg.

"I really think I've had enough rafting for one day," said Rhea. "I'm sunburned and exhausted. Besides, I have to get ready to leave tomorrow."

Don backed off as Trey wrapped an arm around Rhea. "The

interstate's right over there," he indicated. "You can hitch a ride back to Aspen."

"We'll do that," said Trey.

"Are you sure this is what you want to do?" Greg asked.

Both Rhea and Trey nodded. Mona and Chance approached. When they heard the latest turn of events, Mona looked alarmed but reluctantly gave in. She ran back to the raft to retrieve Rhea's daypack. When she returned, she told Rhea, "I won't worry about you because I know you're in good hands."

"Thanks, Mona." Rhea handed over her life jacket, then slung her pack over her shoulder.

"See you at home tonight," Mona called to her.

Rhea watched as the remaining six rafters got back in and floated out of view.

Trey let out a sigh as he sank to the ground again. "Better rest. It's a long walk to Glenwood."

Rhea's teeth still chattered and she hugged herself for warmth. "Thank you for saving my life," she said. "You *did* jump out on purpose, didn't you?"

Trey propped himself up with one elbow. His hair was wet as he smiled, then reached over to draw her close to him. "You're still shivering. Come here."

Rhea welcomed the heat of his body against hers. At last … at last she was in his arms again. It felt wonderful. She closed her eyes and rested her head against his strong shoulder as his hand moved to caress her back. She could feel his heart still pounding from the exertion.

"Trey …" She opened her eyes and saw the river racing by them.

"Hm?"

"Before we head back, I need to tell you something."

Trey held her, but said nothing.

"I'm sorry for the way I acted at your house," said Rhea. "You were right. Parker never told me he was …" She couldn't say it.

Trey broke away from her and picked up a stone to throw into the water. "Let's just forget it," he said.

Rhea was silent. For a while it had seemed as if things

between them had returned to normal. Now she was no longer sure. Something still bothered Trey. What was it? Was it Parker? Was he afraid it would happen all over again? Parker had a way of starting trouble between them every time his name was mentioned. How could she convince Trey that Parker was finally at peace?

"What time is it?" asked Rhea.

"Don't know," said Trey. "I didn't wear my watch. But by the way that sun's starting to move behind the canyon, I'd say it's almost three." He stood up. "Come on, let's see if we can get to the interstate."

Rhea could see the interstate from where they were, but she knew they would have to cross the river to get to it. Behind them was a road that probably led to the interstate. When she pointed this out to Trey, he agreed they should start along it. Slowly they weaved their way among rocks and weeds and ducked under some barbed wire to cross a field that would take them to the back road.

"I'm sorry I ruined your rafting adventure," said Rhea. "You didn't have to quit on my account."

"Well, I wasn't about to just leave you there on the river-bank," said Trey. "Besides, I had my fill of that Don guy."

After they reached the road, Rhea asked, "Do you think any-one travels this road? Maybe we'd be better off swimming across the river."

"Too risky," said Trey. "Someone is sure to drive by and pick us up."

They headed in the direction from which they had come on the raft. For the longest time no cars passed in either direction. Then they heard one approach and Trey stuck out his thumb. The car whizzed right by.

"Strike one," said Rhea.

Half an hour passed and no one stopped, even though three vehicles came by. Rhea sat down in the shade of a tree to rest.

"I never knew hitchhiking was such a bother," she said.

"Don't worry, we'll get to the interstate," said Trey.

"Here comes a truck." Rhea stood up as an old dented yellow pickup crept toward them. To her relief it slowed, brakes squealing, and pulled to a halt beside them. An elderly man in a rumpled hat looked out at them. He had a ruddy complexion and squinty eyes and his chin was stubbly.

"Can you take us to the highway?" Trey asked.

"Where ya headin', young fella?"

"Aspen."

"Get in," the old man responded.

"Thank you." Rhea grabbed her pack. She and Trey climbed into the cab. Her nose was immediately greeted by the over-powering smell of whiskey. She stuck the daypack between herself and the driver and leaned against Trey as he slammed the door shut.

The old man let out the clutch and the truck slowly rolled down the road. He reached under his seat and drew up a bottle of Scotch that was almost empty. He swallowed some, then offered it to Rhea and Trey.

"No, thank you." Rhea turned to Trey, who smiled in amuse-ment. He patted her knee as if to reassure her. Rhea decided that as long as the old man stayed at fifteen miles an hour there was probably no danger, but she didn't like the situation one bit.

"Where ya headin'?" the old man asked again.

Trey explained how they had been rafting and had decided to return to Aspen before their friends.

"Aspen, eh? Pretty place." The old man began rambling about how he preferred staying away from cities like Aspen. "Too much vice," he grumbled as the truck swerved from side to side. The more he talked, the worse his driving became, but he stayed at a relatively slow speed.

"Shouldn't we be turning left?" Trey interrupted as the truck turned right onto a gravel road leading away from the direction of the interstate.

"Bosh!" the driver grunted.

Rhea cringed at his foul breath.

"We want to get to the highway," Trey reminded him.

"This is the shortcut," the driver slurred.

Rhea glanced at Trey, who took her hand in his. "Maybe we should get out here," she said. "We can walk to the highway. It can't be that far ..."

"No you don't!" the driver protested. "Don't deprive an old man of his good deed of the day." Suddenly he picked up speed and the truck swerved and jolted. The bottle of Scotch appeared from beneath the seat once more and the old man took a long swig, nearly losing control of the truck.

"I want to walk," Rhea said. She was scared and clung to Trey.

"Just hang on." Trey squeezed her hand. "We better not get him upset." He cleared his throat. "Thanks for the ride, sir, but this is where we get off."

The old man appeared not to have heard. He turned onto another gravel road and began driving like a maniac. Rhea felt herself being bounced and jolted around. As the truck accelerated, the old man took them onto several back roads. There were no houses. Rhea knew they were far from the interstate now and it looked as if they were in Bureau of Land Management country. Surrounding them was oak brush.

"Trey!" Rhea began to sob as the truck swayed left and right.

Suddenly the driver slumped over the wheel. Rhea grabbed it from under him as his heavy body pressed against her shoulder. The old man had passed out. She struggled to steer as the truck veered right, then left.

"The brake, Rhea! Hit the brake!" cried Trey.

"I can't!" The drunken man's body was crushing her and she couldn't move her foot toward the brake pedal.

Trey leaned over her, completely blocking her view out the windshield. He managed to yank the keys from the ignition and grabbed the emergency brake. The truck skidded dangerously and the pickup jerked to a stop, throwing them forward. They had landed off the side of a dirt road—the truck tilted. Trey wasted no time opening the door. He jumped out and Rhea quickly followed, dragging her pack.

They were in a woodland surrounded by oak brush, pinyon and juniper. Rhea let Trey wrap his arms around her as they recovered their senses. Peeking into the cab, Rhea saw that the old man hadn't moved. "What should we do?" she asked.

Trey sighed. "Even if we had a cell phone, I'm sure it wouldn't work way out here." He looked around, then said, "Let's go for help."

"Should we do something about him?"

"Not now," said Trey. "He's passed out. Let's get out of here before he wakes up."

Rhea followed Trey down the dirt road. They half-ran until they came to another back road. "Which way?" asked Rhea.

"Got me." Trey looked around. "I think we came over that hill."

Rhea wasn't at all sure. She had lost her bearings in the wild ride with the old man. She had been too worried about his driving to pay any attention to directions. With the sun down below the tree line, she couldn't tell east from west. She and Trey followed the road about half a mile and then discovered it ended in a horse trail.

"I guessed wrong," Trey muttered.

"Maybe we should go back to the truck," suggested Rhea. "We could drive it somewhere a lot faster than on foot." She looked at the sky. "It's getting pretty late. The sun's really low."

"What would I do without a sensible lady along?" Trey smiled and they started back toward the truck.

When they reached the road where they had left the truck and the old man, they were startled to see that the pickup was no longer there. They approached the spot and studied the tread marks in the dirt where the truck had come to a halt. Trey reached down and lifted the empty bottle of Scotch.

"He's gone." Rhea looked around and suddenly felt desolate and a little frightened. For a long moment they both were silent. Then Rhea turned to Trey. "What are we going to do if ..." She gasped. "What if I don't get back to Aspen tonight? I'll miss my flight in the morning."

Trey stood up and dropped the bottle. "We must be miles from the interstate."

"Trey, do you have any idea where we are?"

"Lost."

Rhea frowned. They started back down the road. Trey thought perhaps there might be a building or a sign somewhere, but all they saw was more oak brush and trees. "I think we're on

BLM land," she told Trey. Her skin prickled from sunburn and she was tired and thirsty.

"I'm not even sure what direction to go in," said Trey. "If there was a mountain in view, I might be able to get a fix on where we are, but with all this oak brush around ..." He sighed. "I still think our best bet is to head east."

"We were really stupid to leave the truck," said Rhea.

"Come on," said Trey.

The air had turned cool and daylight was fading when they stopped for a longer rest. Rhea was too tired and miserable to talk. She suspected Trey felt ashamed about leaving the truck. They had no water, no warm clothing nor matches. No means of staying warm once the sun set. Rhea knew how cold it could get in these mountains toward the end of summer. She realized it was time to come up with some serious ideas about their survival.

"How long do we have till sunset?" she asked.

Trey studied the pink sky. "I'd say less than half an hour."

"Ever build a fire without matches during one of your horse-back trips?" was Rhea's next question.

"No, but I suppose Parker taught you that as well." Trey's words were laced with sarcasm.

"Will you please forget about Parker?" Rhea stood up and glared at him. "Unless we do something soon, we're going to be in serious trouble. For your information, this happens to be the 30th of August ... and snow storms are not unlikely at this altitude this time of year."

Trey chuckled at the thought. "Snow storms? Not at five thousand feet."

Rhea pouted. "You're making fun of me."

Trey reached for her. "Hey, I'm sorry. You're scared, aren't you, honeybabe?"

Rhea trembled. "Well, it looks like we're going to be stuck out here overnight. Look at how we're dressed—you're in shorts! What if we don't live to see August 31st?"

Trey wrapped his arms around her to calm her. "Rhea, I'm just as worried as you, but we're not going to freeze to death, if I can help it. We'll keep going. There has to be shelter somewhere."

"Where? This is BLM land!"

"Bear with me," he pleaded. He gazed into her worried face. "And I dang well intend to live to see tomorrow. I'd sure as hell hate to be found dead on my birthday."

Rhea stared at him. "Your birthday is tomorrow?"

"That's right."

Rhea hung her head. "Oh, Trey, I'm thirsty and hungry, and my feet are killing me. I'd give anything to be home right now ... in my nice warm bed."

"And I'd give anything to be right there with you." He smiled as she caught the wink in his eye. Then together they started out again. Rhea stopped after a minute. "What's wrong?" asked Trey.

She looked up at him, then lifted her face toward him. He drew her body against his as their lips met in a powerful and passionate embrace. Then she drew back and said, "Happy birthday, Trey ... in case we don't make it."

16

"*I* think there's something ahead," Trey called out in the growing dusk.

Rhea roused her weary body after a five-minute rest. With the sun gone, the evening air had grown chilly.

"It looks like a shelter of some kind." Trey grew excited.

"Where?" Rhea stumbled toward him and Trey caught her hand and pulled her along.

Rhea could make out the silhouette of a building. Even if it turned out to be the remains of an old mining shack, she would welcome anything right now. As they approached she saw another four-wheel drive road that wound toward the building.

"It's a cabin," Trey announced.

"What's it doing way out here?" asked Rhea.

"You never know. It might be a hunting cabin."

"Or maybe it's a ski hut," Rhea added.

"Well, I doubt they'd mind if we put up for the night here." Trey tried the door and found that it opened. "Too far out to have to worry about locks," he commented.

An ashy odor greeted them as they stepped inside the dark room. Rhea shivered and strained to see. Trey groped around and knocked something onto the floor.

"Somebody set up housekeeping here at one time," said Trey. "Here. Throw this on."

Rhea caught a dusty wool blanket that Trey tossed in her direction. She wrapped it around her shoulders and stood still as Trey explored the room in the dark. "Be careful," she told him.

"Hey, there's a stove," he said. "All we need now is some wood and something to light it with."

Rhea edged closer, following Trey's voice. "Maybe they left some matches by the stove."

Something crashed to the floor again and Trey swore out loud.

"Are you all right?" asked Rhea.

A moment later a spark of light illuminated Trey's hand in the tiny flicker of a cigarette lighter. They soon discovered a stack of pinyon wood next to the stove and within minutes they had a fire burning. The wood fire provided more light, enabling Rhea to see what was in the one-room cabin. A small oak table and some stools had been pushed against a wall. An old brass bed took up the opposite wall. It was bare except for a mattress.

"All the comforts of home." Trey fed a few more sticks into the stove.

Rhea explored and discovered some blankets and dishes packed in crates. She took off the blanket now that the fire was starting to heat the room. She knew if this was a hunting retreat—or somebody's private hideaway—it was unlikely they'd have left any food. Nevertheless, she went through the boxes and found sweaters, long underwear and some old *Field and Stream* magazines.

"Rhea!" Trey called out. "Here's something to drink." Trey produced a box of rose hips tea containing three teabags.

"But we don't have any water," she reminded him.

"Maybe there's a water source outside,'" said Trey.

"I wouldn't bet on it."

Trey started for the door. "I'll be right back." He grabbed an empty pot lying on the floor.

In the silence Rhea sat down on the bed and stared out the cabin's only window. She could see the penetrating blue light from the moon and the silhouette of trees on surrounding slopes. She whispered a prayer of thanks that they had found shelter, no matter how decrepit and isolated it was. Blankets and a warm fire were a far cry from spending a cold night out in the open. Aside from the rumblings of her stomach and her parched throat, Rhea knew things could be a lot worse.

She thought over the day's events and wondered if Mona was

home by now. No doubt her roommate would be worried and a search and rescue party would be summoned. The thought made her shudder as she remembered that Parker had once been the subject of search and rescue. Rhea shook the haunting memory away and stared out the window. What was taking Trey so long? Where had he gone? She began to worry that something had happened to him.

The next moment Trey stepped inside the cabin with a cry of triumph. "Water for tea, pretty lady." He brought the pot over to the stove.

Rhea got up from the bed. "Where did you get it?"

He explained that there was a spring not far from the cabin. He offered the pot for her to drink from before he set it on the stove to boil. When her thirst was satisfied, Rhea wiped her lips. A draft blew in and Trey went over to close the door. Then he spread more blankets onto the bed so they could huddle there beside the stove.

"Looks like you're going to miss that flight after all." Trey rubbed his hands together.

Rhea stared into the flames, soothed by the waves of heat and the changing orange shapes that leaped and swayed, consuming the pinyon. "You're right," she replied, then added, "but at least I won't miss your birthday."

"I didn't want you to go anyway," said Trey.

Rhea said nothing. The past week she had dreaded having to go, but the last couple of days she had finally resigned herself to the fact. Nothing had changed. As comfortable as she felt here beside Trey, he couldn't solve her problems for her. Wasn't he also in a financial plight now that he no longer worked for Nickelson Creek Ranch? And even if he asked her to live with him in order to solve her rent problem, how could she expect an arrangement like that to last? Sooner or later he would lose interest in her and she couldn't bear the thought of suffering like she had when he had gone off to Texas to see his girlfriend. Trey was not like Parker. She was sure he preferred to remain a free spirit, no matter how much it had appeared that he cared for her.

"Why *are* you going away?" Trey asked when she didn't

answer him.

"Nothing to keep me here," she replied. "The Music Festival is over. Summer's over and I have to get on with my life."

Trey sighed. "It doesn't have to be over, you know."

"I can't go through another winter in Aspen," Rhea said. "Don't you see? I'm tired of scrounging for a living." She looked at him. "I'm not like you. I can't *be* everything like you are. I do one thing well and it doesn't seem to be enough."

"You mean, you play the piano."

"Exactly."

"Then go on playing the piano."

"Not in some sleazy bar," she objected.

"Then come live in Snowmass."

"Rent is just as high there as it is in Aspen," said Rhea.

"Then don't pay rent."

Rhea couldn't look at him. "Are you asking me to be your live-in lover?"

"No."

Embarrassed, Rhea turned away. They were silent for a few moments. The fire flickered playfully on the walls of the cabin.

Finally Trey spoke. "Did I tell you about my new job?"

"Oh, you found something? Well, I'm happy for you."

"Are you?" Trey asked doubtfully.

"Why shouldn't I be?"

"I think you're upset with me."

Rhea didn't admit that it was really herself she was upset with. "So tell me about your new job," she said.

"Called up my old buddy, John Dowd, the outfitter."

"And he's taking you back?" Rhea forgot her embarrassment from a moment ago. "Oh Trey, that's wonderful!"

"Huntin' season starts soon," said Trey, "and this winter we're gonna do cross-country ski tours."

Rhea stood up as the sizzle of boiling water prompted her to make tea. "I'll bet John was glad to get you back," she said. "He seems pretty nice to work for."

"Who said anything about *workin'* for him?" Trey handed her a couple of chipped cups they had found in one of the boxes. "I got John Dowd workin' for me now."

"Oh, really?" Rhea chuckled as she poured the water into the cups. She'd play along with his joke. "Were those the conditions you demanded when he decided to hire you back?"

"Yeah, it may take some gettin' used to, that's for sure," said Trey. "But this would have been John's last season if I hadn't bailed him out."

Puzzled, Rhea handed him his cup of tea. "What do you mean?"

Trey grinned. "You're lookin' at the new owner of the Nickelson Creek Ranch."

"What?" Rhea spilled some of her tea.

"Watch it, honeybabe."

Rhea steadied her cup. "What are you saying? The new owner?"

"I bought the outfitter business from John Dowd."

"But, Trey ... how?"

"I planned to break the news to you when I got back from Texas, but I had a few things to iron out first. I really didn't know how the deal was gonna turn out till this week."

"Where did you get the money to buy Nickelson Creek Ranch?" Rhea was astonished as she realized Trey was serious.

"Well, I'll tell you," said Trey. "Do you remember that little trip I took to Texas?"

How could she forget? Rhea turned her eyes away in humiliation.

"Well," resumed Trey, "it turns out I came into a bit of money. That's how I was able to buy the ranch."

Rhea closed her eyes and began shaking her head as visions of the rich girlfriend flaunting her cash and buying favors from Trey flashed through her brain. "I don't believe you, Trey."

"Why not?"

"I thought I knew you better than this."

"What's wrong?" He reached for her, but she pulled away from him, disgusted. "I thought you'd be happy for me."

"Well, you thought wrong." Rhea stood up and walked across the room.

"Honeybabe, what did I say?" He set his cup down and followed her.

"Leave me alone."

"I don't understand ..."

"Oh, don't insult me with your false innocence!" fired Rhea. "I knew about it all along. I only kept quiet because I cared about you, even though it hurt so much to think about you and that ... that *floosy!*" Rhea started to cry.

"What floosy? What in tarnation are you ...?"

"Chance told me! That insensitive creep couldn't keep it to himself, you know. It just rolled off his tongue ... you flying to Texas to see your ... your *girlfriend!* And as if that wasn't bad enough, you had to lower yourself to take money for it!"

Trey grasped hold of her and tried to tear her hands away from her face. "Get a hold of yourself, lady. Listen to me!"

Something in his voice commanded her to silence. Rhea opened her eyes and saw that Trey was calm. She waited in anguish for his excuse.

"Rhea, the only reason I told Chance that was so he'd keep his nose out of my affairs." Trey's eyes were fixed on her. "Now I ain't gonna deny there was ever a girl. There were plenty. Even in Texas, for sure ... but I'm tellin' you, I didn't go there in July to spend time with someone else—not when I would rather have stayed in Aspen with *you*. Believe me, I didn't want to go at all."

"Then why ..." Rhea sniffled and settled down a little. "Why didn't you tell me the truth?"

"I couldn't talk about it then." Trey stared at the gritty floor, obviously troubled. "It was on account of my old man."

"Your father?"

Trey nodded. "That's right. You see, the old man and I haven't seen eye to eye since the day I decided to leave home. He wanted me to go to college and then run the company for him so he could retire. I refused. Said I had a life of my own to live. I didn't want to spend the good part of my life being the head of a Texas oil company. Well, when I left, he cut me off and said as far as he was concerned, I was no son of his."

"Trey, I'm so sorry."

"Anyway, my parents bought the house over in Melton Ranch," said Trey. "I didn't tell you that because I didn't want to think of him as my father. My mother arranged for me to stay there and watch over the place." Trey sighed. "Then the old man fell seriously ill in July. His heart gave out."

Rhea looked up at him in sympathy.

"He told my mother he wanted to patch things up with me," Trey resumed, "so she sent the money for me to fly home. I didn't know what to expect. I was so afraid things would grow worse. My dad passed away three weeks later."

"Trey, I wish I had known."

"He was a hard man to get along with," said Trey, "and I may have been wrong to take off the way I did, but at least we had those last weeks together. I saw a side of my father I didn't know existed."

Rhea smiled at him.

Trey took her hands in his and looked into her eyes. "So, honeybabe, I've got this big house in Snowmass and a ranch down-valley. And I don't want to end up like my old man, never appreciating any of it. Yet I'd throw it all into the Roaring Fork River if it would change your mind about leavin'."

Rhea didn't know what to say. All that time she had wasted—stewing over his absence—and instead, he had been suffering with a dying father he hadn't seen in years. She hadn't given him a chance to explain, she had been so wrapped up in her own despair over Parker.

"Stay in Aspen," Trey implored.

Rhea let herself fall into his embrace and he held her close, his form in the dim firelight so tantalizingly male.

"I've never felt like this about any woman before," Trey told her. "Since that first day I saw you, in the grocery store—looking so pissed in the express lane."

Rhea smiled at the memory. "You were the last man on Earth I'd have gone out with," she confessed.

"But you took the chance," said Trey. He slid his hand underneath her shirt and began lifting up her swimsuit bra. Rhea's breasts awoke to his warm touch. His fingers moved in slow hot circles over each nipple, bringing more senses to life.

"When I saw you that first night in the bar," said Rhea, "I was afraid of you."

"I know," Trey murmured, "but somehow I realized that night that my bar-hoppin' days were comin' to an end. Rhea, I don't want anyone else." He kissed her then. "I need you," he said.

Rhea felt a rush of passion surge into every fiber. She knew something was happening over which she had no control. And she didn't want to stop it. She only knew—rich or poor—Trey Michaels was the man she loved and wanted to spend her life with.

His lips found her neck and traveled down her shoulder, sending prickles of delight throughout her body.

"Trey, there's one thing you should know," said Rhea.

"Only if it's that you love me," he replied. "I don't want to hear anythin' else."

Rhea moved aside. "I think our tea's getting cold ..."

"Forget the tea." He led her over to the bed.

"There's something else," said Rhea. "It's about Parker."

"Aw, gosh dang!" Trey cried. "Here we go again!"

Rhea grabbed him and pulled him down on the bed on top of her. "Parker's left," she said. "He'll never come between us again."

For a moment Trey stared at her uncertainly. Then he asked, "He tell you that?" Slowly a smile began to form at the corner of his mouth.

Rhea sighed. "Does it matter?"

"You *do* love me," he said.

"Yes."

"And you won't go away?"

"Not tonight. We're stuck out in the middle of nowhere, remember?"

"But I'm not just talkin' about tonight," said Trey.

"Shhh ..." Rhea put a finger on his lips. Trey said no more as she lay back with his arms around her. The strap to her swimsuit came unclasped and Trey gently removed her pants, then pulled off his shirt and flung it across the room. He kissed her fervently as his body pressed closer against hers.

As his kisses grew deeper, rousing her to readiness, Rhea felt a willingness to submit that she had never known before. Together they rolled on the bed in the deserted cabin, completely swept up in the urgency and passion of the moment. Rhea finally experienced what it was to know the splendor of womanly fulfillment.

Later, as they lay silently side by side, Rhea's heart beat loudly and sweat covered her nakedness. She closed her eyes, secure and warm in Trey's arms. She never knew she could love someone this much. And Parker had not crossed her mind once.

17

*W*hen morning dawned, Rhea awoke beside Trey. The air felt chilly, but they had wrapped themselves in blankets. Their body heat had kept them warm long after the stove had burned out. She was surprised to find Trey staring at her.

"Oh, I must look a mess." Rhea pulled the blanket over her face.

Trey tore the cover away. "If this is the way you look when you wake up in the morning, then I've got somethin' to look forward to the rest of my life."

Rhea smiled at him. "Are you saying what I think you're saying?"

"Well, I sure as hell ain't givin' you the brush-off." Trey kissed her. "Marry me. I'll buy you a piano."

Rhea laughed. "You will?"

"Hey, I'm good for it."

"In that case, how can I turn down an offer like that?" She cuddled against him. "Besides, who could deny you anything when it's your birthday?"

"If you mean that, then how about grantin' me my birthday wish?" Trey reached over and kissed her. A moment later, desire overcame them both and they made love once again.

Afterwards, they lingered in each other's arms a while, then got up and got dressed. Rhea wandered outside the cabin while Trey searched inside, in case any dehydrated food or canned goods had been tucked away by the owners. She was returning from a grove of trees when she heard the sound of a motor not far away. A Jeep with a man and woman in it drove up alongside the cabin and jolted to a stop.

Rhea's first thought was that the owners had come and

would accuse herself and Trey of trespassing. She hurried over to explain their situation just as Trey stepped out of the cabin.

"Hello," called out the man in the Jeep. "Are you from the rafting party?"

"Yes!"

"Thank goodness, you're alive!" cried the woman.

"You two all right?" asked the man. He told them that he and his partner were members of the county search and rescue team. They had been searching along the river most the night.

"Somebody recalled there was an old hut out this way," the woman said, "so we started out as soon as it got light. Nobody figured you'd wander off this far from the river, but I'm glad we took a chance on it."

Trey explained what had happened as Rhea ran inside the cabin to get her daypack. She looked around one last time, then closed her eyes as she basked in her newfound happiness. For a moment the relief swept throughout her entire being and she saw that the world was an exciting adventure once again. She clutched the pack to her breast.

"Rhea, you ready?"

She turned and smiled at Trey in the doorway, then followed him to the waiting Jeep.

"Where are we anyway?" Trey asked as he helped Rhea into the back of the vehicle.

"Flatiron Mesa."

Rhea clutched Trey as a shiver ran through her.

"What's wrong?" he asked.

"Flatiron Mesa," she murmured.

Trey wrinkled his brow. He didn't understand.

She looked into his face. "I never thought I'd have to see the area where Parker was killed." A wave of emotion rippled through her.

"Put this around her." The woman tossed a down coat to Trey, who drew Rhea close as she huddled against him.

"Don't think about it," said Trey.

"No, it's all right." Rhea didn't say it out loud, but a warm feeling came over her. She closed her eyes and saw a vision of Parker's smiling face.

"You're in good hands now," he told her in his gentle voice.

"I'm moving on now. If you ever need me, I'll be close by."

Trey took Rhea's hand in his and squeezed it. "It's all over now, honeybabe. We're goin' home."

Rhea opened her eyes. *Home.* The word suddenly took on new meaning. Rhea leaned against Trey's shoulder as the Jeep bumped over the grassy trail that led away from Flatiron Mesa and toward their future together.

About the Author

Ann Ulrich Miller lived in Aspen and the Roaring Fork Valley of western Colorado in the late 1970s and early '80s. Having been born and reared in the Midwest, the move to the Rocky Mountains had a significant impact on her life.

It was at that time that the seeds of spiritual awakening began to sprout. Aspen and its beauty and diversity of thought encouraged her to explore many different belief systems.

She worked for the *Aspen Times* and the *Snowmass Village Sun*, and in 1984 left with her Forest Service husband and their two young sons to live in Corvallis, Oregon for ten months. When they returned to Colorado in June 1985, they resided in Delta, and their third son was born in November of that year.

From her earliest years music was important in her life. She started piano lessons at the age of 4 and is grateful to her parents for encouraging her musical studies all the way through high school, which included French horn in band and orchestra.

Writing and publishing have dominated her career, however, and her interest in spirituality led to her metaphysical magazine, *The Star Beacon*, in print since 1987.

Under the name Ann Carol Ulrich she has published a sci-fi/romance series (*Intimate Abduction, Return To Terra* and *The Light Being*) as well as a series of young adult novels set in the late 1960s. Currently she has 20 titles in print, in an assortment of genres, and resides in western Colorado, where she continues to write romantic suspense under the name Ann Ulrich Miller, including *Rainbow Majesty*, which was a Finalist in the 2015 Eric Hoffer Book Awards.

www.annulrichmiller.com

ROMANTIC SUSPENSE

"A captivating, page-turning story of intrigue and romance."
—Judith Horky, author of *EarthShift*

RAINBOW MAJESTY
Where Love and Light Converge

A novel by **Ann Ulrich Miller**

"This memorable tale will move you to tears, inspire you with hope, uplift you with joy." —John Cali
Great Western Publishing Co.

Struck down by her fiancé's death in Iraq, and now the loss of her long-suffering mother, a young woman searches for the meaning of life.....

Hoping to seek answers to her father's death 22 years prior, Juniper Sutton leaves Kansas for the Rocky Mountains. Converted from a hunting resort, the Rainbow Majestic Lodge now caters to light workers and Juniper agrees to manage the lodge's new gift shop for her Aunt Rosalee.

Two men employed by her aunt capture her heart while she is thrust into a new way of thinking and encounters extraordinary people and ideas. But Gena Sutton Howard, Juniper's first cousin, sets herself up from the beginning to challenge Juniper every step of the way. However, Gena's psychic ability uncovers something she'd rather not know about the young woman from Kansas, and the lodge's dark secrets begin to spill out — even to the point of *murder*.

"In Rainbow Majesty, *Ann Ulrich Miller has masterfully woven richly drawn characters, suspense, love and self-discovery into a captivating story. Readers for whom this is an introduction to spirituality can understand its presence in their own lives through the characters' experiences, and already enlightened readers will applaud the clarity of universal truths throughout this greatly enjoyable book."* — Suzanne Ward, author of
Matthew, Tell Me About Heaven and other Matthew Books

RAINBOW MAJESTY
ISBN 978-0-944851-32-6
280 pages, paperback
$15.00 USD + $3.50 S&H
Also available at **Amazon.com** and Create Space
www.createspace.com/3455770